"Keep running!"

Overhead, Zeke could hear the helicopter circling, looking for signs of Susanna. All he could do now was pray that they were hidden from sight as they plunged deeper into the forest. The denser the canopy, the better hidden they would be. But Susanna was wearing bright blue and white—she'd stand out.

Zeke ran until his lungs were on fire and his feet felt like lead, and he was mostly carrying Susanna as she stumbled along behind him. Then he stopped against a thick trunk and pulled her with him against it, both breathing hard. At least they wouldn't be seen overhead.

"The helicopter is landing by the blind," Zeke said, his breath coming in heaves. "They're checking if we were inside—if we're dead..."

"Who are they?" Susanna wheezed. She leaned over, her hands on her knees.

"I have no idea, but they're pulling in all of their resources," he said.

"For me..."

He didn't answer. But yes, it was all for her. What did they think she knew? And why this one Amish woman?

Patricia Johns is a *Publishers Weekly* bestselling author who writes from Alberta, Canada, where she lives with her husband and son. She writes Amish romances that will leave you yearning for a simpler life. You can find her at patriciajohns.com and on social media, where she loves to connect with her readers. Drop by her website and you might find your next read!

Books by Patricia Johns

Love Inspired Suspense

Grave Amish Secrets
Innocent Amish Target

Love Inspired

Amish Chocolate Shop Brides

An Amish Baby in Her Arms
An Amish Bookshop Courtship

Amish Country Matches

The Amish Matchmaking Dilemma
Their Amish Secret
The Amish Marriage Arrangement
An Amish Mother for His Child
Her Pretend Amish Beau
Amish Sleigh Bells

Visit the Author Profile page at LoveInspired.com for more titles.

INNOCENT AMISH TARGET

PATRICIA JOHNS

LOVE INSPIRED® SUSPENSE
INSPIRATIONAL ROMANCE

Recycling programs for this product may not exist in your area.

ISBN-13: 978-1-335-95782-5

Innocent Amish Target

Love Inspired
22 Adelaide St. West, 41st Floor
Toronto, Ontario M5H 4E3, Canada
www.LoveInspired.com

HarperCollins Publishers
Macken House, 39/40 Mayor Street Upper,
Dublin 1, D01 C9W8, Ireland
www.HarperCollins.com

Printed in Lithuania

1 2 3 4 5 6 7 8 9 10 LIT 28 27 26 25

But the Lord said unto Samuel, Look not on his countenance, or on the height of his stature; because I have refused him: for the Lord seeth not as man seeth; for man looketh on the outward appearance, but the Lord looketh on the heart.

—*1 Samuel* 16:7

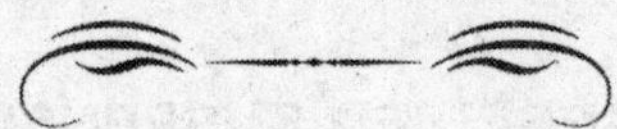

To my husband and son. Thank you for all of your support as I hammer out my stories and for your help with all the extra things in the running of a small business. You make everything sweeter, and I love doing this together. I love you!

ONE

Susanna Stutzman looked over her shoulder as she crossed the street, shopping bags in both hands. The day was bright and sunny, a few clouds scudding across the June sky. But she was eyeing the blue van that was parallel parked along the curb—it was there when she began her shopping and it hadn't moved. The driver wasn't even looking in her direction. He was bent over his cell phone, but her pulse sped up all the same.

She was being ridiculous. She was in broad daylight in the middle of town, but after what had happened to her cousin, nothing felt safe. The police officers who talked to them after delivering the news had suggested grief counseling and personal therapy to help with precisely this problem. But the Amish leaned on each other, not Englisher medical folk.

And most importantly, they leaned on Gott.

Gott, protect me...

They might not lean on Englisher medical professionals, but Susanna did sometimes wish she had someone who could tell her that her new anxiety was both misplaced and normal. That would help her to feel better.

She stepped up on the opposite curb and headed down the street. The bags were starting to dig into her palms, and she was eager to get them loaded up into the buggy. She was finished her shopping for the week, and it was time to head back to the house. Times like this, she wished she'd worked a little faster to turn the old family house into a bed-and-breakfast. At least she wouldn't be alone in those rambling rooms anymore.

Susanna looked over her shoulder again. The van hadn't moved, but it did seem like the driver was looking at her now.

"It's just my imagination," she murmured aloud.

She turned down the side street that led to the buggy parking lot. Her hands were getting sore from the heavy bag handles. She was tempted to stop for a moment and rest, till the sound of an engine roared up behind her. Her heart leaped, and she spun around in time to see the blue van's sliding door whip open and a man jump out. It all happened so quickly that her mind was still catching up when he grabbed her by her arm. He heaved her toward him as a scream escaped her lips. A strong hand slapped over her mouth, another dug into her upper arm, and dread settled into her belly.

"Police! Freeze!" a voice shouted.

Whoever was holding on to her startled, and Susanna bit down on a foul-smelling finger that was pressed against her lips, and she jerked out of his grip. He swore, shaking his bloodied finger while his gaze stayed locked on her face for one terrifying second, a slight sneer turning up his lips. The iron taste of blood was in her mouth, and she could feel his loathing as he smoothly jumped back into the van. Susanna's body suddenly snapped into motion, and she started to run.

She didn't get far. A figure appeared in front of her, and she bounced of him, sending her backward. She stumbled and stared up at a large, steely man who stood with a gun drawn and aimed at the retreating van. He didn't look like police—there was no uniform, just jeans and a polo shirt. He was tall, with dark hair and a no-nonsense way about him. He used both hands to steady his weapon as he aimed, then muttered something and lowered it.

"Are you okay?" he asked.

His hands were big and square—reassuring, like a farmer's hands. Susanna's eyes were locked on the gun, though, and he holstered it. He only spared her a glance as he pulled a small notebook out of his pocket and jotted something down. She wiped her mouth and her hand came away with a smear of blood on it. Her stomach gave a heave, and she spat on the ground. She had to swallow hard against the rising bile in her throat. She leaned forward, her head spinning. Was she about to empty her stomach?

"I'm sorry to scare you," he said. "Are you hurt?"

"No." She spat again.

"I'm Detective Zeke Esch from the Pennsylvania State Police."

Susanna put her hands on her knees, trying to get her balance back. She looked at her dropped bags—sugar and flour strewn across the pavement in a wave of white and a spattering of dried beans mingling with the gravel. Only a bag of canned goods remained intact. Tears welled up inside of her.

"Are you okay?" he repeated.

"No," she said, her voice shaking.

Susanna bent and tried to pick up her groceries, and the detective squatted down next to her and gathered up the bag of cans and the bag that had what was left of the flour and sugar. Susanna brushed at a pile of sugar on the sidewalk, already attracting a line of ants.

"Leave it," he said.

He was right, of course. Someone would have to come with a broom.

"Come on," he said. "I need you to tell me everything that happened. Did you know that man?"

She shook her head. She'd never seen him before in her life.

"Stick close to me." Zeke led the way back toward the main street, but she noticed how his gaze raked the area, taking in their surroundings. "You'll be all right."

She didn't need to be told twice, her heart still hammering in her chest, and she fell in at Zeke's elbow, hurrying back to the busier main street.

"What's your name?" Zeke asked.

"Susanna Stutzman."

"That's a common last name."

"*Yah*, I suppose."

"Well, I need you to tell me everything, Susanna," Zeke said as they reached the sidewalk. "Everything you can remember, no matter how small or insignificant. It's important that we do this now, while everything is fresh in your mind."

"Who are you again?" Susanna asked.

Zeke pulled out his badge and held it up for her to see. "I'm Detective Zeke Esch. State police."

It looked official enough, not that she'd know the difference anyway.

"I can take you back to the station right now—" he started.

"No." She swallowed hard, taking a step back. "I'm not going anywhere with you."

She wasn't getting into any cars, vans or even buggies with anyone right now! Who had that man been? What had just happened?

"Okay…fair." Zeke met her gaze and for a moment he just regarded her quietly. He was tall, broad shouldered, and he had kind eyes. She hadn't noticed his eyes before this. But he did look like a safe sort of man. Not that she even trusted her own instincts right now. He was tall, with tousled mahogany-colored hair, and a cleanly shaven face. He had broad shoulders and strong hands—and he was reassuringly polite.

"How about we sit in that diner?" Zeke pointed up the street. "We'll sit by a window, and you can leave whenever you want. No pressure. But I need to know what you remember so we can catch that guy, okay?"

Susanna looked up the street. It was in public. The diner he was indicating was Amish owned and operated, so she'd be around her own people.

"Okay," she agreed. She looked down at the blood on her hand and she was about to scrub it off when he caught her hand.

"If you don't mind, I'd like to take a sample of that blood. We can link it to your attacker. Proof."

"Oh…"

He pulled out a handkerchief and wiped the blood off her hand, then carefully folded it up and pocketed it.

"Let's start with what happened," he said as they walked toward the diner.

She told him what she could remember—walking down the street, noticing the van, turning down the side street and the van suddenly whipping up behind her.

"Have you noticed that van around town before today?" he asked.

"I don't think so. But there are always delivery vans and that sort of thing. And I notice Englisher vehicles ever since my cousin died."

"I knew I recognized your last name. Is your cousin Hannah Stutzman?"

"*Yah.* She was murdered three weeks ago." Her voice shook. "They found her body in a dumpster in Lebanon."

"I'm so sorry. We've been investigating her murder."

Hannah had left the community a couple of months prior to her death, and when a police officer had come to her parents' door to give the heartbreaking news, nothing was the same again.

"Do you know why she left the community?" he asked.

"Her parents didn't say?" She'd thought that her aunt and uncle had explained all this to the police.

"They thought she wanted to experience the world."

"She had an Englisher boyfriend," Susanna replied. "Why do most girls leave?" She'd begged Hannah to stay. Hannah had claimed her beau was the kindest, dearest, most besotted man on the planet. But he wasn't Amish. And he wanted her to marry him. So much for that. Hannah hadn't lived long enough.

"From what we understand, she was baptized?" he asked. "I mean…was she shunned for leaving?"

He seemed to understand the Amish culture, and she frowned. "Esch. Are you from the Amish Esches?"

"I am. My family was Amish until I was fourteen. So I understand the shunning process pretty well."

"Okay, then. Well, she hadn't already joined the church, but her *daet* is a deacon, so *yah*, she was shunned," Susanna said. "At least she wasn't welcome back home until she properly confessed."

"Did you meet her boyfriend?" he asked.

She shook her head.

"How did she meet him?"

"He was a friend of a friend. Something like that. They met at a party, I think, and they hit it off."

"Were you ever at those parties?"

"I don't drink," she said. "And I don't go to those kinds of parties. So no, I never saw him. Hannah and I were almost the same age. We were born the same month, and our mothers were very close. But we were different as night and day. Hannah was outspoken and she challenged everything. And I love our faith and our way of life. I didn't want the freedom she wanted."

"One other girl from this community was abducted, but she got away. Do you know her?" he asked.

"Rachel Lapp. She's about three years younger than me."

"Was she going to those parties, too?" he asked.

Susanna shook her head. "No, she didn't go to those parties. She was courting with a nice Amish boy. No one was supposed to know, of course, but I caught her holding hands with him behind a barn one Service Sunday, and that made it clear enough. She never would have gone to those parties and jeopardized things with Abram Zook. When she was taken, she was walking from church back to her grandparents on a Sunday afternoon, and she never made it. She managed to get away and she flagged down a car that took her to the police station. Normally we don't go to the police, but that shows you how scared she was. She's still a wreck."

"Someone is targeting Amish women out here. There have been other abductions in other communities, too."

"But Hannah looked as English as you do."

Zeke opened the diner door for her and let her go inside first. He put a hand in front of her as a young Englisher man brushed past them to leave the diner. She was glad for his protective gestures. Right now any man within reach of her made her pulse speed up.

He led her to a table by the window and pulled out a chair for her, then took a seat opposite her that gave him a view of the door. When the waitress came with two glasses of ice water, he said, "Tea?"

It would do. Susanna wasn't sure she'd keep anything else down.

"One cup of hot tea," Zeke said. "And maybe a piece of pie."

The waitress left, and Susanna looked around nervously. Zeke dipped a napkin in the glass of water and took her hand, dabbing the blood away. She was grateful—she felt a little more like herself with a clean hand.

"You're safe," Zeke said quietly. "I'm not letting anyone touch you. Okay? When I'm here, you're safe. I promise you that."

"Okay…" It did make her feel a bit better. Zeke had a competent look about him, like he could make good on that promise. She took a sip from the other glass, cleaning out the foul taste in her mouth from the man's finger.

"So you said you've never seen that van around here before?" he asked.

"Not that I noticed. It's pretty ordinary looking, though. The flower shop has a van a lot like it. And there's a plumber around here that's got a blue van, too."

The waitress returned with the tea and pie. She put the tea in front of Susanna with a worried look on her face, and a slice of banana cream pie in front of Zeke. But when the waitress left, Zeke slid the pie in front of Susanna.

"You might be able to eat a bite or two," he murmured.

"Danke." She took a sip of tea, and it did have a settling effect on her stomach.

"So it sounds like this was a crime of opportunity," Zeke said quietly. "They saw a young woman walking alone, her hands full, and when you passed into that side street, they knew they had you cornered."

A shiver slid down her spine.

"Look, it's not necessarily connected, but since I've been working on your cousin's case, I'd like to get a few details we haven't nailed down yet. What was Hannah's boyfriend's name?" he asked.

"Shawn Neufeld."

Zeke jotted that down.

"I remember because she kept writing her name out as it would be when she married him."

"Did she marry him?"

"She didn't live long enough." Susanna felt the tears rising. "But she would have. She was so in love with him. They were talking about having children and how they'd raise them."

"So there's a grieving fiancé out there?"

"I suppose."

"Did he contact her parents, or any of the rest of you?"

Susanna was silent, her mind spinning. "No, Shawn didn't contact us. He didn't come to her funeral, either."

"Did that strike you as strange?"

"Considering she was running away from us to go live with him, I didn't think anything of it. He wasn't welcome in her parents' home. Besides, her parents thought that if she'd just stayed at home, she'd still be alive. Maybe he didn't want to be blamed."

"I've seen a lot in this job, Susanna," Zeke said quietly. "I don't know who killed your cousin, or if all of the attacks are connected yet, but I do know that whoever is doing this isn't going to stop."

"What am I supposed to do?" she asked. "I'm a woman living alone. My father died last year, and I live in a house by myself. I work at the grocery store."

"You could let me bring you into police custody while you think about your next step," he said. "We'll get the local police to up their patrols and warn the community."

She shook her head. Custody. Getting into a car with a strange man. No, she wasn't doing it.

"Let me talk to my boss," Zeke said.

"Who's your boss?" she asked nervously.

"He's the station chief in Jonestown," Zeke said. "I'm actually not on the job right now. I'm supposed to have a couple days off. Let me just see what he thinks we should do."

Susanna nodded. Her head was still spinning. Whoever had been kidnapping women had now targeted her, and if Zeke hadn't stepped in when he had, she might be in the clutches of some very evil men.

Two personal days. That was all Zeke had asked for. Two days off. So much for a chance to have some privacy with his own emotions for a couple of days. His Amish grandfather whom he hadn't seen since he was a young teen had passed away and the old man had written in his will that his youngest living grandson should have his house. That was Zeke. The will had been made long before Zeke was even born. Had his grandfather forgotten the wording of his will?

So Zeke had an old house to put in order in a conservative Amish community outside the town of Felder—just a few miles from here. He'd stopped in Treue to use the restroom and he spotted that van turn down a side street and heard a scream that curdled his blood.

Susanna was a pretty Amish woman with thick brown hair pulled up into a bun under her white prayer *kapp*, and expressive dark eyes. When she fixed him with a direct look, it sparked an instant protectiveness inside of him.

Zeke held his cell phone to his ear while he got his earbud connected, then he put the cell phone face up on the table in front of him and pulled out his notebook. He jotted down a couple of notes from the things Susanna had told him. Her name, her connection to Hannah Stutzman, and this mysterious man named Shawn who simply evaporated as soon as Hannah turned up dead. Shawn Neufeld—how many men by that name were in the vicinity of the towns of Treue and Felder in Lebanon County? Probably a few. Plus there were the Weaverland Mennonites, who might have some Neufelds, too. It was a place to start. Zeke had read Hannah Stutzman's file, and no one had said as much as Susanna just had. As a rule, Amish people didn't like law enforcement. They didn't trust them.

He made the call and Chief Hernandez listened as Zeke described what had happened.

"I was able to get the license plate number of the van," Zeke said. "Although I'm willing to bet it's forged or stolen." He read it off.

"Give me a minute," the chief said, and then came back a moment later. "The plate number is assigned to a pink Volkswagen bug in Philadelphia, and it's not reported stolen. So either the plate is a forgery, or the owner doesn't know the plate is missing yet."

So that was a dead end.

"The victim didn't recognize her assailant," Zeke went on. "But she has a connection to another abducted and murdered woman. She's Hannah Stutzman's cousin."

"Hannah Stutzman..."

"She's one of my cases—a deceased female found in a

dumpster in downtown Lebanon. Her family is Amish and lives in the Treue area."

"Right." The chief sounded serious. "And now the dead woman's cousin has been attacked, too. Do you see any connections between the two besides relation?"

"It's too early to tell, sir."

"Is it possible this isn't just a convenient snatch?" the chief asked. "Maybe there's someone connected to both women. That's quite the coincidence, and you know how I feel about coincidences."

"I do, sir, but she's scared out of her mind right now," Zeke said, and he met Susanna's wide-eyed stare. "I do have one piece of evidence. She bit him when he tried to snatch her, and she got some of his blood on her lip. I took a sample."

"Good for her! I like a fighting spirit. And good catch getting the sample. We'll have to get that into the lab ASAP. Maybe we can get a match and issue an arrest warrant."

"It's worth a try, for sure," Zeke agreed. "But here's the thing, Chief. She's right here with me, and she lives alone. She's vulnerable."

"Esch, she isn't a witness to her cousin's murder who can give us any information," the chief replied. "You thwarted the attempted abduction, and we currently have an escaped inmate from the county prison. He didn't return from work release, and we're stretched thin as it is with a manhunt. I'd say to get her safely home and make sure she knows who to call if anything else happens."

Zeke was silent for a moment. "You're right. I'll do that. Thanks, Chief."

Ending the call, he met Susanna's questioning look.

"I wanted you to hear my side of the conversation, at least," Zeke said. "I need you to be able to trust me."

Getting an Amish woman to trust him as a cop was an uphill climb, and he knew it.

"What did your boss say?" she asked.

"He suggests that I take you home and make sure you know how to contact us if anything else happens."

She nodded mutely.

"And you say you live alone?" he asked.

"I do."

"Is there anywhere I can take you where you'd be with family or friends? I'd suggest that you not be alone right now. Even if nothing else happens, you're going to feel pretty spooked."

There was no more reasonable threat to her right now—not that he could back up on paperwork, at least. But he couldn't leave her alone until she'd made some safer plans.

"My siblings moved away before my *daet* died. And most of our extended family is in Lancaster County," she said. "I have one aunt and uncle in our community—Hannah's parents. They're grieving right now over Hannah, but I'm sure they will let me stay with them until I can figure out a better solution."

"That sounds like a good idea," he said. "At least you won't be alone then. I'll leave you my contact information in case you need anything at all."

"I've got my horse and buggy still in the parking lot. I need to bring them home."

Of course... He'd have to file a report and make sure the local police knew about the attempted abduction so they could be on alert, and then he'd be on his way again to his grandfather's Amish community, and his own business that he needed to take care of.

"I can follow you back in my car," he suggested.

Susanna smiled for the first time, and her solemn expression suddenly bloomed into heart-stopping beauty. His breath caught. Wow. She had a smile that could stop traffic!

"*Yah*, that would work," Susanna replied, and she picked up her fork and took a bite of the banana cream pie.

A few more hours, and Zeke would be on his way to his family's Amish settlement outside the town of Felder once more. But something didn't sit right about this whole situation. Those men had tried to snatch a woman in broad daylight, and while he'd chased them off, they hadn't been easily spooked, either. His gut told him that they were professionals. And with all of the women going missing lately—and not turning up dead—Zeke and his team were already suspecting human trafficking. Susanna's attempted abduction might not be connected to Hannah's death at all, but he knew one thing for certain. These creeps in the blue van would come back.

Would Susanna's plan to stay with her aunt and uncle be enough?

TWO

Susanna looked in her buggy's side mirror at the car creeping along behind her as she made her way up the winding road that led home. Zeke Esch was a different sort of man. He was large and obviously strong, but he had a gentle way about him, like a farmer she'd met when she was a girl. The man had had a way with kittens.

She halfway wished she had him next to her in the buggy, but the plodding of the horse's hooves and the warm summer sunlight were comforting in their own way. She sent up another prayer for protection and guidance. Ever since Rachel's abduction and Hannah's death, nothing had felt normal. Maybe it never would.

But Gott had protected her from some dangerous men today—there was no other explanation. Gott had sent this Englisher police detective into the little town of Treue at just the right moment. If Zeke had not shown up when he had, she shuddered to think of where she'd be right now.

She might be dead like her cousin. Or worse.

She didn't live far from town. The family farm that she'd inherited had been sold off to neighboring farms piece by piece until the house on an acre was all that remained. Her brothers and sisters had moved away—two going English and moving to Pittsburgh, and the others simply unable to afford the pricey farmland in Lebanon County, so they'd moved out to Ohio and Oklahoma to join small Amish communities out there. That left Susanna on her own in the family house with church leadership constantly concerned about her. Maybe she could appreciate their concern a little better now.

When she pulled into her drive, she looked around at the trees, the brush, the lawn that needed mowing again… Home. This was the house she'd grown up in, the house where both of her parents had passed away—her mother when she was twelve, and her father last year. This house held so many memories, and she'd hate to leave it. Would she find a way to come back again?

She might need to be married first! That was one point the local bishop was pushing for. He didn't think a woman should live alone, and if she wasn't living with family, he'd want her married.

But for her own safety, would Susanna have to leave Pennsylvania completely? Because she couldn't stay with her aunt and uncle for long. She was a grown woman now, not a child. And who in her immediate family would volunteer to take her? If she wanted to stay Amish, she'd have to go to Ohio or Oklahoma. She wouldn't have a lot of choice. This was why she had opted to live alone.

Zeke followed her down the drive and then parked next to the house. He got out of his car and looked around, his gaze like a razor, swiping around the property. Then he approached her buggy as she was hopping down.

"How long are we staying?" he asked.

"Do you mind if we eat some lunch before I pack?" she asked.

"Sure," he said. "We should let the horse get some rest, then. I'll give you a hand."

"Do you remember how?" she asked.

"I'm sure it'll come back to me."

She studied him out of the corner of her eye. He'd been raised Amish, so this wouldn't be too foreign for him. She kept looking around as they unhitched the horse, and when the sound of an engine on the road drew their attention, she heaved a sigh when it was just a pickup truck that carried on past without slowing.

They circled around to start undoing the straps and buckles. He was right—he did know what he was doing. His hands were strong, and he worked faster than she did, then came around to her side of the horse, taking the last buckle from her fingers to finish it. His hand was warm and calloused, and she felt some warmth in her cheeks at his casual touch.

He might have been Amish until he was a teen, but he didn't seem to remember how Amish folk behaved between men and women.

Susanna only had the one horse. She bought milk and eggs from the grocery store she worked at in town so she didn't have any other animals to care for, and it did cut down on the chores around here.

When they had the horse settled in the pasture, Susanna led the way into the house.

"Are you hungry?" she asked. Because she was.

"*Yah*, I am," he replied. That was the Pennsylvania Dutch coming out in his speech, and she understood where it came from now.

"A nice vegetable soup and sandwiches would hit the spot for me," she said. "What do you say?"

He nodded. "Sounds great. What can I do to help?"

"Just don't get in the way," she said with a smile. She preferred to have him across the room, anyway. It made things a little more comfortable. She hardly knew him, after all, and now he was in her house and they were alone. This was highly improper by Amish standards. She should have the neighbor here or a friend or a cousin—

Her throat closed off at the sudden memory of Hannah. Hannah would have gladly stepped in to make sure things were proper, all the while casting Susanna little rebellious smiles. She was like that.

"Can I show you some pictures?" Zeke asked. He had his phone out, and he held up a photo that looked like a mug shot of a middle-aged man.

"Who is that?" Susanna asked.

"I just need to know if you recognize any of these people," Zeke said. "I want to see if the man who tried to snatch you is someone already known to us."

"I can look," Susanna replied.

"*Danke*," he said—the Pennsylvania Dutch coming out in his words again. "How about this man?" She shook her head. "This woman? Have you seen her around?"

She shook her head again.

Zeke worked through fifteen or twenty mug shots, and she hadn't recognized anyone. She turned back to the cooking, but as she did, she noticed some movement outside the kitchen window. She froze, waiting to see if it would happen again.

"What did you see?" Zeke asked softly.

Then a squirrel jumped up onto the windowsill, and she startled, then laughed uncomfortably.

"Just a squirrel, I guess. They rob my bird feeders."

Just a squirrel… Was she ever going to feel safe again?

"Can I ask you something?" she asked.

"Sure."

"The police said they'd let us know if they found out anything about Hannah's killer. Did you learn anything at all?"

"Nothing more than I've already told you. The address on her Amish ID was her parents' place, and she obviously no longer lived there. We had no way to track down that boyfriend, so I'm glad we now have his name, at least," he said. "Most of our evidence came from her body. After the autopsy, all of those samples from her body were sent for testing. They were put in line behind a lot of other samples from other cases. These things take time, unfortunately. Quite a bit of time. If we can catch up with Shawn Neufeld that would be a great help. He might know more—give us an idea of someone who might have been spending time with her, earning her trust."

She nodded.

"Giving me his name is really helpful," he reiterated. "And anything else you might be able to tell me. We find that Amish families don't like to tell us much. But the more information we have, the better we're able to do our jobs."

"We keep secrets," she murmured.

"I know."

"I mean…about our romantic relationships. When an Amish boy and girl are dating, it's a big secret. If they've been together long enough, people figure it out, but dating happens after dark, and it's supposed to protect reputations. Don't you remember this?"

"I wasn't told much about dating. I wasn't old enough to do it. But yes, I do remember the secrecy around who was out driving with whom."

"It's how we do things. So Hannah wouldn't say anything to her parents about Shawn. And they'd never expect her to. I was the one who told them she'd been dating Shawn after she died. They had no idea."

"So we questioned the wrong family members," he said.

She shrugged. "Hannah didn't tell many people about Shawn."

"But she told you."

"We were close."

"Did anyone from the police question you?" he asked.

"They asked a few questions when they told us about her death."

"And you didn't tell them about Shawn?"

Susanna shook her head. "My cousin trusted me. And I didn't think it had anything to do with her murder."

Zeke met her gaze thoughtfully, and Susanna felt some heat in her cheeks. She didn't like feeling inspected like that. She turned away with the excuse of putting the food on the table.

"Sit down," she said. "Have some lunch. It's the least I can do to thank you."

After a silent grace, they both started to eat, but halfway through the meal, the sound of an engine on the drive pulled Zeke out of his chair. The engine turned off, and Susanna swallowed her bite of sandwich with difficulty.

"It's a blue van," he whispered.

Susanna felt her heart hammer to a stop. How? Had they followed them back? How could they possibly know where she lived?

Zeke held up a hand, and she held her breath. Zeke moved soundlessly from one window to the next, staying behind the curtain. He froze, his hand out behind him in a silent gesture for her to get down. Susanna slipped away from the table and crouched down behind the cupboard. There were footsteps, then a polite knock at the rear door that led into the kitchen.

Zeke shook his head at her, and she didn't move. Her

breath sounded loud in her own ears, and she eased open a kitchen cupboard and wrapped her fingers around the handle of an iron skillet. Another knock—a bit louder this time, but still sounding quite polite.

Zeke's gaze flew around the room—he looked in the direction of the front door, then at the staircase.

"*Yah?* Who is it?" Zeke asked loudly, sounding awfully Amish to her ear, and probably to whoever was outside, too. Maybe with a man here, they'd just go away. Zeke went toward the door, but he stayed back and to the side.

"Hello?" a man's voice called. "We got a flat tire. My wife is pregnant, and she's really tired and overheated. Do you think you could help us?"

Was it really just a pregnant woman in need of help out there? Just another blue van by happenstance? But then the knob rattled. People seeking help didn't try doors.

"Could you help us?" the man asked from outside. "My wife needs help. She's pregnant—"

Yah, he'd mentioned that already.

Zeke pulled his gun out of the holster at his side.

But then suddenly there was a splintering bang, and the door crashed open. A scream lodged itself in Susanna's throat as a tall, burly man burst into the house and lunged at Zeke.

Zeke ducked and threw himself backward. He moved before he even thought, his training coming back in a rush. The big man's swipe missed him, and Zeke whipped his leg across the other man's ankle, bringing him down with a crash.

There was a flurry of fists and grunting as he struggled for dominance against a much larger opponent, his heart hammering in his ears as he fought, his stomach turning at the smell of sausage and onions on the man's breath. It was a series of defenses and attacks, and at some point his gun went spinning across the floor out of both of their reach.

For a minute or two, Zeke thought he might have the upper hand, but then the man landed a solid punch that made Zeke's head explode in pain and the room spin. He found himself flat on his back, the heavier man straddled over his chest so he couldn't move or fight, and that ham of a fist coming toward his face.

He'd almost given himself up to the inevitable knockout when something big and heavy hit the man in the head with a hollow clang. His attacker swayed for a moment, his fist fell, and then he toppled to the side. Zeke looked up at Susanna standing there with an iron skillet in her hands, her chest heaving.

"Did I kill him?" she gasped.

Zeke rolled over, pushing himself to his feet and grabbing his gun. He squinted against the pain in his head and looked down at the large man, spread-eagle on the floor. He was breathing but likely in need of medical attention from the heavy blow.

"He's fine," Zeke replied. No need to worry about him right now. "But that was good aim on your part."

There were boots coming up the step, and another man appeared in the doorway, and footsteps could be heard coming in the front door.

That was both ground level exits blocked off, and with an assailant coming at him, he had one path available to him. Grabbing Susanna's arm, he hauled her with him toward the stairs. She bolted into action and they both scrambled up as fast as they could go. But Susanna took the lead when they hit the upstairs hallway and opened a small door that looked like a closet. It was not—it was a tiny bedroom with one small window.

Zeke pushed a sliding bolt lock into place just as a body plowed into the door, making the wood creak under the pressure.

"Open this window," Susanna whispered, and she heaved against the old, swollen wood. Zeke joined her, and together they hoisted the old window open as wide as they could. Just beneath the window was a thick tree limb—their way out!

Zeke couldn't see anyone outside, the three men—including the one who was unconscious—all seeming to be in the house, and the conscious two now throwing their energy into breaking down the door. As the sturdy wood held in place, there came a gunshot—they were going to shoot it down now.

"Go!" Zeke whispered, and Susanna eased out the window and onto the tree limb.

It wouldn't hold up both of them, so he had to wait until she got closer to the trunk of the tree while bullets splintered the wood and gun reports echoed behind them. Her feet slipped as she scrambled toward the trunk, and Zeke crawled out onto the limb as the door behind him bowed with another blow.

God, protect us!

That door wasn't going to last, and Zeke didn't have time to climb. He got a good grip on the limb and hung down, then dropped the last few feet, sending up a silent prayer of gratitude when he didn't roll an ankle. Susanna was coming down the tree, but there were no more footholds.

"Jump!" Zeke whispered hoarsely.

Susanna looked down at him, back up at the window, and then her face paled.

"They're outside!" a male voice bellowed.

"Jump!" Zeke repeated, and Susanna dropped in a fluttering mass of fabric and limbs. He caught her and the wind rushed out of her lungs as she connected with his chest. He lowered her to the ground.

"You okay?" he asked.

"*Yah!* I'm fine!"

A gunshot rang through the air and the ground right next to him exploded in a shower of dirt. Grabbing Susanna's hand, he zigzagged across the yard toward the trees. Susanna was a little slower than he was, but not by much, and he was grateful for that.

"Stay low and move fast!" Zeke ordered. "They'll never hit us in these trees. Just keep moving!"

They actually might be able to shoot them through the trees, but they'd be a much harder target than running through the open field.

A bullet splintered a tree behind them, and Zeke kept running, his lungs burning. "This way!"

He needed to get to the car. On foot, they'd have little chance of escape, but in the vehicle, they could make a proper run for it. They moved into denser foliage, and he could see two large men dressed in gray and black standing in the grass, guns raised, and looking around. They had that laser-focused look of men with military training. One lowered his gun and muttered something that looked foul.

They can't see us, he realized in a rush. Good! That was helpful.

"Stay low and quiet," he whispered close to her ear, and he pulled out his key fob. "When we reach the car, jump in and lean down. They're going to shoot."

God, shield us! he prayed, because he knew the odds, and they weren't good. Those men were going to turn and aim the second they heard a noise. But he didn't have much choice. If those men got their hands on Susanna, it would be worse. Men with military training attacking some unknown Amish girl—there were limited reasons they'd do this, and none of them were good. Hannah had been executed—fast, efficient, cold-blooded. By these people, or others? They were the same type. He'd seen a lot in the last few years. Zeke's breath was ragged in his throat, and he waited until the men turned away, looking back toward the garden, and then he exchanged a look with Susanna.

Run, he mouthed.

And they ran.

Susanna pulled open the door of his sedan and dove in, and Zeke circled around and had just gotten into the driver's seat when a bullet shattered the back driver's side window. It took a couple of tries to get the key in the ignition, then he turned it, the engine came to life and he stepped on the gas.

"Buckle up!" he shouted, and Susanna reached for the seat belt, still leaning down.

Zeke sped down the drive, shooting gravel out behind the wheels, and as he spun onto the road, he spotted the van in the rearview mirror.

"They're coming!" Susanna gasped.

"Yep." And they wouldn't stop. He knew it in his gut. Zeke could see the van coming up hard behind, and he reached for his own seat belt and snapped it into place. He pulled out his phone and voice dialed 911.

"This is Detective Zeke Esch of Troop L of Pennsylvania State Police," he said as soon as the operator picked up. "We are in a high speed pursuit. We are on—" He looked over at Susanna. "Where are we?"

"Hudson Road leading toward the highway."

Right. That was it. "We're on Hudson Road leading toward Route 322. We need police backup. I have a civilian with me and she is in imminent danger."

There was no answer, and he picked up the phone and looked at it with a quick glance—the call had dropped. These back roads could be iffy with cell phone reception.

"Siri, call 911!" he barked.

The phone started calling but dropped again. Now the van behind them was gaining, and Zeke tossed his cell phone into the cup holder next to him. Susanna turned around, looking back wide-eyed.

"It's okay," he said, reaching out and taking her hand.

Susanna squeezed his hand back hard and, for a moment, they felt completely connected, his heart beating in rhythm with hers. He was going to get her out of this—that was his vow to himself. He would get Susanna out of these people's reach, and he'd put as many of them as possible behind bars. The memory of Susanna's face when that animal was trying to drag her into his van was forever seared into his memory. The fear in her eyes, the revulsion, the panic. And when they'd crashed into her house, he'd known that this had been no coincidence. They'd known where she lived. Now he was certain she needed protection.

There was one firm belief that Zeke had kept from his Amish upbringing, and that was a certainty that God's hand was in everything. God was still with him, and God wasn't done yet.

They were approaching the highway now, and the van behind him started to increase its speed. Zeke did the same, putting his foot down to the metal, but this was his own personal Toyota, not a squad car with the extra power and bulletproofing.

Even with his gas pedal stamped flat, that van kept closing the gap. He wasn't going to outrun it, was he?

"Okay, your seat belt is on?" Zeke asked.

"*Yah*," Susanna said breathlessly.

"Once we hit the highway, I'm going to brake," he said. "That van has more power than we do, and I'd rather not be pushed off the road."

He checked his mirrors again, and the vehicle behind gave another burst of speed and started pulling up on his bumper, then it crept up beside him. This was bad…really bad! Had the 911 operator heard enough? Was there backup coming? He couldn't hear sirens, and the highway merging lane was upon them.

The van was coming up close beside them, and Zeke's first thought was of a gun. If that window got parallel to him, he and Susanna were both as good as dead, so he couldn't let that happen.

Just then, the van's side panel door unlatched and started to open, and several things occurred to Zeke in a split second: first of all, that driver wasn't alone in that van; secondly that whoever was opening that door was going to shoot straight into his window; and thirdly, that his choices had just run out.

He stamped on the brakes, and Susanna jerked forward, restrained by her seat belt. The tires squealed, and the back end of the van clipped his front bumper. The impact pushed his passenger side tire over the lip of the road onto gravel, and suddenly, the road in front of them started to rotate, and they were turning in the air like a rotisserie chicken. The only thought left in Zeke's mind was a prayer that came out in his mother tongue.

Gott protect her! he prayed in Pennsylvania Dutch.

And then they landed with a crunch and the shatter of glass.

THREE

Susanna blinked her eyes open. Everything was upside down, and her head felt light and very heavy at the same time. Her weight was pulling her downward toward the roof of the car, her seat belt holding her into her seat. She could smell the scent of gasoline, but stronger than that, she could smell smoke. She squirmed, but when the shoulder strap started to slip off her shoulder, she stopped. A ringing in her ears drowned out everything else, and when she looked in Zeke's direction, terrified she'd find him injured or worse, she saw him gazing at her earnestly through a veil of gray smoke, his lips moving, his eyes red with irritation. He was talking to her.

"...do you hear me?" was the first thing she registered, and she nodded.

"Good," he said. "I'm cutting our seat belts, and we need to get out of here. Do you smell that?"

"*Yah*," she said. It smelled like a bonfire out in the back field. She remembered they'd use gasoline to start the blaze when the day was wet. "It's on fire."

"Exactly." He pulled a folding knife out of a pocket, and he sawed away at his own seat belt first. When he cut through the last of the tough material, he dropped to the roof of the car, putting his hand out to protect himself. He had to work himself around so that he was on his knees, and then he reached up and sawed away at her belt next. She put her hands out to catch herself, and found herself face-first on the ceiling of the car. Zeke was already squirming out his own broken window.

"Follow me," his muffled voice said. "There's more room on my side."

She squirmed after him, broken glass cutting into her palms and elbows, but then Zeke caught her hands and helped to pull her the rest of the way out. As she lay panting in the ditch, smoke billowed out of the windows. They'd only barely made it out before all of the air would have been gone. She could see the van ahead, stopped in the middle of a highway lane, and she looked behind her to a spread of trees close by.

"Run," Zeke said, his voice a growl in her ear, and without any further urging, she scrambled up the incline and dashed on wobbling legs toward the trees. She flung herself into the underbrush and found Zeke landing next to her. She looked back toward the car as orange flames erupted.

The van reversed then, and the door opened, two men jumping out. Just as the men approached the car, there was a deafening boom as the car exploded. The men shielded their faces against the roaring blaze, and backed up. They looked around the ditch, then up at the trees, then back at the blaze.

"They think we're in there," Susanna breathed.

"They do," Zeke agreed. "And that's a good thing. If they think we're dead, they'll stop looking for us."

Who else would think they were dead, though? Would the police? Would her family and friends? Her heart gave a squeeze, and Zeke's warm hand pulled her back out of her emotions.

"My phone was in there," Zeke said, and he sounded more annoyed than anything. "So we're on our own for the time being. Let's get moving. I don't hear sirens yet. Either the operator didn't hear enough, or law enforcement is still on their way. If we stay here, those men will come find us. We have to put some miles between us and that van."

She nodded numbly. He was right, of course. The longer they stuck around, the more likely they'd be found by the wrong people.

"We've got to move quietly and keep low," Zeke said, meeting her gaze, looking for her understanding. "Okay?"

"Okay." Susanna got to her feet, crouching down. "Let's go."

Zeke might expect her to fall apart under the pressure, but she wasn't that kind of woman. Blood dotted her palm from the broken glass, but she couldn't feel any shards left in her flesh, so she'd heal.

Zeke caught her good hand in his, and they headed off deeper into the woods and farther from the smell of acrid smoke. His grip was firm and warm, and next to him, she felt safer.

The trees grew denser as they pressed farther into the forest, and twice they stopped and listened—nothing but the twitter of birds and the odd crackle of a mouse or rabbit in the underbrush disturbing the quiet. The bugs were worse deeper into the forest—buzzing, biting insects flying at her face. She was glad for her dress that covered much of her skin, but her neck was still vulnerable, and she slapped at a biting fly.

"Do you know where we're going?" Susanna asked.

"This area is so densely farmed that if we keep going in one direction, we'll hit farmland eventually," Zeke replied. "And we're heading due west."

"Toward Felder?" she guessed. "These woods are full of insects."

"I know. Sorry."

"Can't we get to a road?"

"I'm thinking if we can get to my grandfather's house, maybe my extended family out there will help us. Even if not, there's shelter, food and a door that will lock. Back when I was a teenager, my grandfather kept a phone in the barn for his business. It might still be connected. No one will be looking there."

"Not even the police?" she asked.

"Not even them. I asked for some personal days. I didn't tell them what I was doing with them."

"But if the police find us, we're safe, right?" she asked.

"We are. I'm thinking we head for Felder, and if we can find a phone hut on the way, we can call for help," he said. "But we'll need to stay away from main roads."

"Why? They think we're dead."

For a moment, Zeke was silent, then he sighed. "For some reason they seem incredibly fixated on getting their hands on you, and you have only me to protect you right now. Just me."

"And Gott," she whispered.

"And God," he agreed. "True. But we're avoiding main roads." The last words brooked no argument.

"Okay. Agreed," she said.

This was worse than she thought. Why on earth were these people focused on her? What had she done to draw their attention?

Oh, Gott, protect me!

She was reminded of the biblical David's psalms when he was running for his life. But she wasn't as eloquent as him. All she had inside of her was a deep and frightened prayer. *May Gott protect us from evil men.*

The trees thinned, and they could hear the sound of babbling water before the creek became visible. She hurried toward it and bent down next to the fast moving water and washed her hands, then rubbed them over her face and neck. The cold water was a relief, and she looked upstream. She didn't know what she expected to see as proof that the water was safe.

"I'm thirsty," she said.

"Me, too, but we'd better not drink this stream water," Zeke said. "We have no way to boil it, and this stream probably runs through farmland at some point. We don't know what's in it."

Susanna was parched, her mouth feeling sticky, and looking down at sparkling, running water and not being able to take so much as a sip didn't help. But Zeke was right. Her older brothers had gotten incredibly ill from drinking from the wrong water source when hunting one year.

"Our first goal is going to be to find water and some shelter," Zeke said. "Do you know this area at all?"

"*Nee*," she said. "Not personally. But I think this is near some hunting grounds my brothers used to use. They came out this direction."

"I think it's better to keep going due west toward Felder."

"What I really wish we could do is circle back around and go back to my community. But we'd only be putting my friends in danger, wouldn't we?"

"Apparently, these people know where you live," he replied. "And if they have a reason for wanting you in particular, they're going to be watching for us to do just that."

It was out of the question. She'd seen what they tried to

do at the house. What would they do to someone harboring them?

"You're right. The Felder Amish community has your family connections, an empty house, food, water and shelter," Susanna said. "It's much more promising."

He looked over his shoulder the way they'd come, then rose to his feet. "It's about fifteen miles between Treue and Felder, and we drove about five miles, I'd guess. That's ten miles left. We'd better keep moving. I don't want to be in the forest when night falls, if we can help it."

Somewhere above them, Susanna heard the chopping sound of a helicopter. She shielded her eyes, looking up. She couldn't see anything in the wedge of sky that was visible, though.

"Is that friendly?" Zeke asked.

"Who would come looking for us this quickly?" she asked.

"I don't know."

The helicopter passed their field of view, and Zeke pulled back, but shaded his eyes.

"Who is it?" she asked.

"It's not police or medical," he said. "Maybe a news chopper? I can't tell."

A helicopter flying over the woods…and pretty low, too, like the occupants were looking for something. Or someone.

"Could it be those men who are after me?" she asked. "Or is that ridiculous?"

Zeke shaded his eyes and when the chopper was within sight again, he pulled her back into the foliage and they stepped behind a big tree. She waited for an answer. She wanted him to say that was an overreaction, a silly thing to even consider. She wanted some sort of reassurance that this would be over soon.

"I don't know. If we're dealing with organized crime, then they'd have access to their own helicopters," he replied. "Criminal organizations have access to a lot of money. Their resources aren't limited. But why would they want you specifically, Susanna?"

Her heart thundered in her chest, and they both looked up again. Whoever they were, the helicopter wasn't directly overhead anymore.

Zeke took the lead, and Susanna followed as they picked their way across the stream and headed into the denser forest. Why on earth would someone be after her? She was a quiet woman living a quiet life. She was the reasonable one. The responsible one. A life lived well within the boundary lines was supposed to be a safe and contented life…so what was happening?

After over an hour of walking, the sun was sinking into the western sky, bright golden rays flickering through the trees from time to time, stretching shadows behind them. It was the golden hour—the time of day when her garden looked like it was bathed in gold, and when the kitchen would be flooded with warm, luminous sunlight. But she was far from home, and in the woods, the bugs were still biting, but the air had cooled and goose bumps stood up on her arms. The sunlight wasn't strong enough after getting through the forest canopy to warm her skin.

Ahead, she spotted something through the trees. She almost missed it, except that it blocked out some glittering golden rays of sunlight, and it was backlit with a glow of afternoon light. It was a small, covered hut about five feet off the ground on stilts and built into the trees. A blind. Zeke spotted it at the same time she did. Her adrenaline had long worn off and she was so tired. Her legs ached, her feet were sore, she was hungry, thirsty and longed to just sit. The blind looked empty.

"Danke, Gott..." Zeke went on to pray softly, and she looked at him in surprise.

"That was in Pennsylvania Dutch," she said.

Zeke startled. "What?"

"Your prayer. It was in *Deutsch*."

He smiled wanly. "It was the language I first learned to pray in. It comes back sometimes."

He was certainly an interesting man—strong, competent, reassuring and layered. But at the bottom of all of that had once been an Amish faith. How much of it was left? she wondered.

"Come on," Zeke said. "Let's see if there are any supplies."

At the very least, they'd just found shelter.

Zeke scanned the area. The blind had a simple staircase leading up to the door. There was a sign on the door that said, "Trespassers will be shot. Survivors will be shot again." It was crude humor, but he smiled ruefully at it, all the same. Here was hoping no one saw them as trespassers here today. He circled the blind once, just to make sure it was well and truly empty.

The structure was made out of barn wood—he recognized it immediately because of the plank size. Barn wood was a one-by-eight plank, and it was probably supplied by the Amish, or it had been repurposed. Sometimes when old barns and sheds were disintegrating, people would scavenge the wood for other projects. It saved money. He headed up the simple staircase and tried the door. It opened with a creak.

Susanna came up after him, both of them stepping into the little hut and looking around.

Three walls had narrow windows that could be hinged open to shoot out of, and beneath each window was a cup holder screwed into the wall. There were some empty beer cans in the corner, and one wall had a glossy magazine photo of a woman in a bikini posing with a rifle. This was definitely not an Amish blind.

"That's going to come down," Zeke muttered. He certainly wasn't going to stare at that picture for the next twelve hours.

"What's this?" Susanna asked, and she opened up what looked like a wooden firewood box, but it didn't contain firewood. There were some cans of food, a box of protein bars, matches, gun oil, a tin pot, a plastic jug and a kerosene lantern with some kerosene in it still.

Zeke sent up a silent prayer of thanks. This was exactly what they'd need to get through the night, plus a few extras. But the most pressing need was water. When he looked out the window, he spotted a break in the trees—a good sign that there was another stream.

He felt Susanna's arm against his as she joined him looking out the window.

"Do you think that might be water?" he asked.

"I think so," she agreed. "We can boil it with that pot if we put together a fire outside."

There was a chill in the air already, and a fire would help with warmth tonight.

"All right," Zeke said, picking up the pot. "I'm going for water. You stay here."

"I can collect some wood," she said.

He shot her a surprised smile. That's right—she wasn't exactly helpless, was she? As an Amish woman, she knew about a lot of things regular Americans didn't, and how to build a fire was only scraping the surface.

"Okay," he said. "I'll be back."

Zeke needed a plan, though. Susanna might be smart and competent, but she was also a target. He had to get her back into state police custody at the station where no one would be able to hurt her. But why were these men after her in the first place? Either she was hiding something, or she really was completely baffled. He was inclined to believe the latter. That left another possibility—she knew something. She might not know what it was, but they did.

Something to do with her cousin's death? Or to do with the other girls' attempted kidnapping? It was a possibility.

The break in the trees did turn out to be a stream—this one faster flowing than the first one they crossed, and he dipped the pot into the stream and brought it up full of sparkling, clear water. He was incredibly thirsty, but they'd have to boil this water and cool it before they could drink it. Then boil more. A good part of this evening was going to be spent on preparing drinking water.

When he made it back to the blind, he found that Susanna had already accumulated some sticks and branches, and she was clearing a spot on the ground to make a fire. He looked overhead. If those helicopters came back, this fire was going to draw attention, but he wasn't sure what else they could do.

Lord, put Your hand over us, he prayed. *Help me to get Susanna to safety.*

Because out in these woods, there were more dangers than just the criminals, and they needed to stay invisible for the time being. There was no way around it.

Zeke put the pot of water on the ground, and then added some dried leaves and twigs to the base of the wood. Susanna struck a match and leaned low to blow. Her *kapp* was dirty now—as was her dress. He looked down at his own clothes—but they were darker in color, so they didn't show the dirt as easily as hers. When they got back into the public, she wasn't going to blend in.

When the fire caught and started to crackle, Susanna arranged two new tree branches in a V.

"I need your knife," she said.

Zeke pulled it out of his pocket, and she accepted it with a smile, her fingers lingering on his hand for a beat. She turned back to her work and peeled a long piece of bark off one branch, then used the bark to tie the two limbs together. She added in a third and did the same until she had a tripod from which to hang the pot over the flames. Then she handed back the knife.

"Once we get enough water to drink, we have to douse the fire," Zeke said.

Susanna looked upward, then back at the fire. "The smoke."

"It can be seen for miles," he confirmed.

She nodded. "Let's not waste a moment, then."

They settled on the ground next to the fire—the smoke that would alert everyone to their presence also acted as a natural bug repellant. But for a few minutes while they waited for the water to boil, it was a relief, and even the hard ground felt good. He caught Susanna's gaze locked on him. When he saw her, she looked down.

"What?" he said.

"You don't look Amish."

"I'm not anymore," he said.

"I know but…" He chuckled when she looked up at him again, this time with more scrutiny. "Maybe I can see it in the chin. How old were you when you left again?"

"My parents left when I was fourteen," he said. "They had some theological differences with the community and they decided to leave and go English. I'd just finished Amish school, so they put me right on into the ninth grade in an Englisher high school."

"How was that?" she asked.

"As bad as you'd imagine," he replied. "I was a farm kid who didn't know how to dress, didn't know anything about pop culture and who missed his Amish life."

"You missed it?" she asked.

"Desperately. But my loyalties were to my parents, and our Amish community near Felder had shunned them. I wasn't going back where they weren't welcome. My *daet* was a good man, and he put his family first always. He worked his fingers to the bone and put everything into making sure we fit into things as best we could. He took me shopping for Englisher clothes and running shoes, but it cost more than he thought it would. So he gave me an Englisher haircut himself with a pair of clippers. I didn't have the heart to tell him that the kids made fun of me every single day for my dumb-looking haircut."

Zeke didn't know why he was talking so much, and he clamped his mouth shut, feeling foolish. She hadn't asked for all that. But truth be told, he hadn't had anyone to talk to in a very long time about his Amish upbringing who'd understand.

The pot started to steam, and he poked at the fire with a stick.

"So you stayed English for your parents," Susanna said.

"I did. I loved them, and they'd already lost everyone else in their lives, and I wouldn't break their hearts by going back."

"You're a good son," she said. "But the bishop would say you should have gone back anyway."

He thought back to his parents' serious talk with him and his siblings. They hadn't given them any option to stay behind. They'd been so earnest, so hopeful.

It will be a new start, and you'll have better opportunities, his *daet* had said. *We'll stay together as a family, and we'll find our way.*

"My family left without me," she said.

Zeke raised his eyes and found Susanna's solemn gaze resting on him. The pain looked old, like she knew how to carry it now.

"Your siblings, you mean?" he asked.

"*Yah*. They all moved away—they couldn't wait to get out to their own adventures. And I was left with Daet. Mamm died when I was twelve, from a stroke. And my *daet* was sick a lot. Something in his lungs, and he refused to see anyone other than the Amish doctor. I was about fourteen, too, when the last of my siblings moved away, and I was left to take care of Daet by myself."

"That's a big burden for someone so young," he said.

She nodded. "*Yah*. It was."

"Why didn't you move closer to your siblings when your father passed away?" he asked.

"You mean last year?"

"Sure."

"They didn't want me." She paused. "I'm nearing thirty, probably will never marry, and I'm just an extra mouth to feed and person to house. I'm an extra woman getting in the way of my sisters-in-law. Don't get me wrong, they asked me to come, but I could hear it in all their voices—they were relieved when I said I wanted to stay in Treue. I'm a burden. You and your parents and siblings—you went to-gether. At least you were wanted."

"Not with my extended family, I'm not," he admitted.

He wasn't so different from her. She was the odd one out with her family, and he was the odd one out with the whole world. He'd never be English enough to really settle in comfortably, and he'd never be Amish enough, either, for his extended family. Even though he wasn't shunned since he wasn't baptized when they'd left, his parents were. And because of that, no one had reached out.

The pot started to boil, and he let it bubble a couple of minutes before they pulled it carefully off the flames to let it cool. Some spilled onto the ground and he grimaced. That was precious drinking water. He poured it carefully into the jug to let it cool.

Looking across the fire at Susanna, he couldn't help but wonder what had dragged her into the middle of this ugliness.

"Here's the thing, Susanna," he said quietly. "I think we can agree that these people are after you. They tried to abduct you in town, and then either followed us to your house, or knew where you lived. And they came for you specifically."

Susanna licked her lips. "Do *you* think they followed us to my house?"

"They could have." He doubted it, though. "But I kept a good eye on my mirrors. I know a thing or two about shaking someone tailing me, and that blue van doesn't ex-actly blend in."

Susanna sighed.

"Or, like I said, they knew where to come for you. Are you sure you don't have any English friends you chat with?

Maybe at work? People who might know where you live, but also might have connections you don't know about?"

"I have coworkers at the grocery store," she said. "But they don't know where I live. I'm not that close to them."

So where was the connection here?

"Did you ever meet Hannah's Englisher friends?" he asked.

"No. She knew better than to bring me along to meet them. I wasn't fun. I wouldn't have gone along anyway. Zeke, I have no idea why they want me! I don't know what makes me special!"

And that was going to be a problem, because until he knew why these people were after her, he wouldn't know how to protect her for the long term.

"I have news for you," he said. "If these people are who I think they are, then going to stay with family, even if they are out of state, isn't going to be enough."

"Who do you think they are?"

"Organized crime. We've been chipping away at their numbers over the years, but they keep growing."

"What could they possibly want from me?" she asked, shaking her head. "I have lived a quiet life in a quiet community. My cousin was the rebel, not me!"

Zeke pressed his lips together, letting his gaze travel amongst the trees as he considered the facts they had so far. She was wanted by a small group of men who were both organized and determined to abduct her. She had no contact with Englisher friends or coworkers who might know where she lived, and she generally lived a quiet Amish life. Her cousin was her only connection to the Englisher world besides some siblings.

"Your Englisher siblings," he said. "How often do you talk to them?"

"I haven't seen them since the funeral."

"But have you spoken to any of them?"

"My brother called and left a message on our answering service. I called him back. That was when Hannah's body was found."

Back to Hannah. She really did seem to be the only troublesome connection Susanna had.

"Tell me about Hannah. Did you communicate with her after her shunning?"

"It was just letters," she said softly.

"Letters?" Zeke couldn't help a little surge of interest. That sounded a whole lot like evidence—and that was what the investigation needed right now. The victim had been sending letters to her cousin? It was almost too good to be true.

"*Yah*, she mailed me letters."

"Do you have them still?"

"I have one. The others I burned. I didn't want to get into trouble with my uncle and aunt. They were really upset with her and wanted her to come home. I wasn't supposed to be communicating with her."

"What did she say in those letters?"

"Just… I don't know. She just chatted. But she never said anything too specific. She was talking about Shawn a lot—how he brought her flowers, how he was going to bring her to meet his mother soon. She said that his mother was going to give her her wedding dress for their wedding day. But then in the last letter she wrote that Shawn had gotten beaten up. He was hurt pretty badly. He lost a tooth and his face was a mess, she said. That one really upset me. She was upset, too. And she would say things about how she was afraid of Shawn's friends."

"Did she mention other people? Any names?"

That wouldn't be admissible in a court of law. Whatever her cousin said in a letter was hearsay. But it might point them in the right direction for an investigation, at the very least.

"Not really. She mostly talked about her and Shawn."

"Did you answer her back?"

"There was no return address. I couldn't. I think she was trying to save me from having to explain myself to her parents. Like I said, my uncle is a deacon."

"So your cousin knew your home mailing address. If the people who killed her got ahold of one of her letters to you, they might have gotten your address that way."

"But why me?"

"Maybe they were afraid she'd told you something that would get them into trouble. Did she say anything that sounded strange, or wrong? Besides Shawn getting beaten up, I mean."

"It was all strange and wrong—she'd left our faith! But no, nothing that sounded like it was against the law or anything like that."

"So maybe it isn't what she actually told you, but what they *fear* she told you."

"What could my cousin have known that got her killed?" Susanna whispered. "And why would she be involved with bad people? I don't understand that."

"We don't know," he said. "Maybe it was a friend of her boyfriend's. She did say his friends scared her."

"*Yah*, she did."

"Shawn would know more," he said. "I'd love to have a chance to chat with him. If he had questionable friends, or if she did, Shawn would be the guy who could point us in the right direction. What else did she say about him?"

"He was sweet. He loved her. They wanted to have a small wedding in the small town where he grew up."

"What town?"

"I don't remember…"

Shawn Neufeld was their key. Zeke felt it in his bones. He was the closest person to Hannah, and somehow they hadn't been able to track him down. Was he a man grieving the loss of his fiancée, or was he more sinister than that?

"What about me?" Susanna asked. "What do I do to get these people to forget about me?"

"All I know is that we need to keep one step ahead of them," Zeke said. "Right now, we have no other choice."

A few minutes later, the water was cool enough to drink—still hot, but consumable. They took turns sipping out of the pitcher, letting sweet water pour down their parched throats. Without even saying as much, they both kept drinking past their thirst, just to make sure the water was consumed and not wasted.

"I'll go refill this at the stream," Zeke said, picking up the pot. "We can have a pot of boiled water in the hut for later."

"*Yah*, that's a good idea."

Zeke tramped off in the direction of the stream, his heart still stumbling over the fact that there had been letters. They had been thorough, but somehow they'd missed questioning the one woman who'd been in contact with Hannah Stutzman. At least he had her in his custody now. But he still had no idea who was after her, or if it was connected to her cousin's death.

He bent over the stream and dipped the pot into the tumbling water just as he heard the far-off sound of a coyote's yipping scream.

He froze, listening. Was this coyote alone? They worked in pairs.

There it was—another short howl in answer farther off, and then another from a different direction. There was more than one pair out tonight. He took the filled pot and headed back in the direction of the hunting blind.

There were coyotes out there—the human kind and the animal—and they would all do the same thing given half a chance. They were scavengers, and with the element of surprise in their favor, they'd kill.

FOUR

The afternoon drifted by, the time passing with boiling drinking water and cooking some oatmeal packets from the storage box in the little shack on stilts. Susanna and Zeke both ate quickly out of the same pot as there were no other dishes to use. Susanna had never gone on her brothers' hunting trips, so this camping experience was a fresh one for her.

"You have the last bite," Zeke said.

"You should." He was the one protecting the both of them, after all.

Zeke handed her the pot without another word, and he watched her pointedly until she scraped the last of the oatmeal onto her spoon and put it into her mouth. Then he took the pot back and trudged off in the direction of the stream again. She could make out his retreating footsteps—the shivering crack and crush of the undergrowth.

Susanna looked up at the hunting blind. It wasn't an attractive building—a shingled roof and barn plank siding. It sat about five feet above the ground on stilts, narrow openings around the top of the building partially opened like heavy-lidded eyes. It wouldn't be comfortable, but it was better than sleeping outside.

The coyote's cries sent shivers down Susanna's spine.

The light grew dimmer in the forest, and it wasn't just her would-be abductors that made her feel as if she had a target on her back. Now the coyotes seemed to be circling in closer and closer. They weren't exactly pack animals, but the sound of several of them still made the hair on her neck stand up.

A cool wind rustled the leaves overhead and she rubbed her arms. For all the heat of the afternoon, the evening was cooling off fast.

Zeke's footsteps came back in her direction, and she could hear the crack of twigs and the rustle of his boots in the undergrowth before she spotted him. He was making noise purposefully—warning off wild animals. There would be more animals out here they didn't want to startle. Like black bears and bobcats. Skunks.

"We'd better get that fire out," Zeke said. "We can't risk being seen from the air, and in the dark, a campfire stands out—trust me on that."

"*Yah*, that's probably true," she said, although she'd miss the warmth of those flickering flames all the same.

Zeke kicked dirt over their fire. The little bit of warm light it had provided winked out, leaving them in twilit darkness.

She looked upward toward the darkening tree canopy. The sky wasn't dark enough for stars yet, and the tree limbs stood out in crooked lines against the velvet gray.

"Let's get inside," Zeke said.

That was a good idea. She normally enjoyed the quiet of the outdoors at night, but not after everything she'd just gone through. Susanna went up the wooden ladder that led into the blind, and she clambered into the little shack and blinked in the darkness. Zeke came up the stairs next, and when he came into the shelter, she was aware of just how limited their space was.

Zeke pushed open the long, narrow openings used for shooting. The low light outside was better than the darkness inside, and it gave Zeke some light by which to get the kerosene lantern lit.

When the lantern glowed to life, Susanna closed the wooden flaps once more, and she sank into a folding canvas chair. Zeke set the lantern on a small table and sat in a folding chair opposite her. The lantern gave off a little bit of heat, and Susanna could feel the space already warming. The bark and howl of coyote pierced the air. She was grateful to be elevated like this, closed off from the wild, even if by some old weathered barnwood.

"Susanna, do you know if Rachel and Hannah knew each other?" Zeke asked. "Is there any connection between them?"

Susanna blinked at him. "I… I don't know. You think the same people who tried to take Rachel were the ones who killed my cousin?"

"It's unlikely," he said. "There have been other girls abducted, and one other besides Rachel who got away—she was in a Weaverland Mennonite community. But normally when girls are being abducted for human trafficking purposes, they keep them alive. Hannah was killed—it doesn't match the pattern."

"And the other girls—" Susanna wrapped her arms around herself, suddenly feeling chilled. "You think they were trafficked?"

"We don't know for sure, but it's highly possible. That is the theory we've been running with."

"Why us?" she asked. "Why Plain girls?"

"Maybe you're simply more vulnerable," he replied. "A

girl walking alone down a country road is a lot easier to snatch without anyone noticing."

"I was in town," she countered.

"Which is different from your cousin, who was killed in the city, and the other girls who were snatched in rural areas." He sighed. "Plus, those men knew where you lived and came after you there. That doesn't match a crime of convenience theory, either. But there are a lot of coincidences, and there is one thing I have in common with my boss."

"What's that?"

"I hate coincidences."

"Why?"

"They aren't as common as people think. Most people see a pattern and some alarm in their brain rings, pointing out that there is a connection, but they don't take it any farther. They call it a random happenstance. 'How weird that those two things should be connected in this one way. Must be coincidence.' But most times there is a connection. Your brain just wasn't noticing something random. It's a pattern, and with some hard work and investigation, we can dig it up."

"Like my cousin being killed and then some gang trying to kidnap me," she said.

"Exactly like that." He pressed his lips together. "And other girls being abducted in Plain communities all over the county when it used to be relatively unheard of for these things to happen in this area."

The memory of those strong hands grabbing her, the taste of that foul finger in her mouth—she tried to push it back.

"What do they do with…us?" she asked hesitantly.

Zeke met her gaze, and she could see something in his dark eyes that held him back.

"If it is human trafficking, it's ugly," he replied. "They normally use drugs to keep the women subdued, and they sell them to the highest bidder."

To use for whatever evil purposes those wicked men had in mind. Her blood froze at the thought.

"But Hannah was in her English clothes," she said. "Right? Wasn't she? She wouldn't have looked Amish."

"You're right. And she didn't have any needle puncture marks on her skin that we could see," he said.

"So maybe it wasn't…that." She couldn't even put it in words—the evil intended for those poor abducted women.

"That's why we didn't assume it was connected," Zeke agreed. "But then Hannah's cousin is targeted specifically, and I have to wonder…why?"

"*Yah*, me, too," she agreed weakly. Why were these men after her?

Outside, the coyote's yipping was getting closer, and then suddenly there was the bloodcurdling scream of a rabbit.

Susanna and Zeke both turned their heads in the direction of that scream, as if they could see right through the walls of the blind, and Susanna shivered. That was the sound of a wild rabbit's death. Death was not easy for any creature on Gott's green earth. Humans were not alone in that suffering.

Had Hannah suffered? That question had been nagging at Susanna ever since her body was found. Had Hannah's last moments been filled with pain and terror? Or had Gott given her some merciful comfort in those last breaths?

She'd heard some gossip about poor Hannah's death— women saying that it was because she left the community that she was vulnerable. Safety was here in the fold. But then Rachel had been nearly abducted, and even their community wasn't feeling so safe anymore.

"I'm sorry if these questions scare you," he said.

"I don't think it can be helped." She licked her lips. "These men are terrifying."

"But they aren't invincible," he said. "They're going to make mistakes. They'll leave evidence behind that we can use to find them. And the more powerful they feel, the less careful they'll be. And when that happens, we'll be ready."

That did make her feel better. "You aren't scared of them?"

"I have a healthy respect for their ability to kill me," he said.

"That's not fear?" she asked.

"That's just pragmatism."

She couldn't help but smile at that, and she shook her head. "What drew you to this kind of work—dealing with these awful things?"

"When I was in grade twelve, one of my friends was beaten up when he was walking home from his job at the gas station," Zeke said. "My family was very sad for him, and said that even in the face of these terrible things, we must ask God to help us to forgive."

Susanna nodded. "That sounds right."

"But he was terrified," Zeke said. "I was scared, too. I mean, it was just a group of local thugs who were joyriding and looking for a good time. They were high, and they got violent. How do you protect yourself from random violence?"

"That's exactly what I'm wondering now," she agreed.

"Well, his family weren't Amish, and they called the police immediately. My friend gave descriptions of the vehicle and he knew who a couple of young men in the group were. The police picked them up and they crumbled under questioning, giving each other up left and right. All five were charged, convicted and two of them did jail time. The other three were given parole with criminal records."

"Oh…" That did feel rather satisfying—consequences for evil actions.

"It was then that I realized I could be part of the solution," he said. "I could actually solve a few problems if I became a cop. There is a verse in the Bible that says that the Son of God was manifested that He might destroy the works of the devil. And while Jesus beat the devil with His death on the cross, until Jesus comes again, the devil is still prowling. And I believe that God is still destroying evil in our lives—and I wanted to be part of that."

"I was ready to disagree with you—because we Amish do not work in law enforcement. We don't fight back."

"I know," he said quietly. "But I felt like I had to. And pushing back against evil to protect the innocent—that felt like God's work."

Susanna had to admit that she felt that much safer with this man who was willing to fight those evil men to protect her. Even though she shouldn't be relying on a man to protect her. She had a Heavenly Father who was more than capable.

Zeke rummaged in the storage box and he pulled out a box of protein bars.

"Let's have one each right now, and then have the rest in the morning," Zeke said.

Susanna accepted one and tore open the wrapper. She was hungry—the oatmeal hadn't been enough. She took a bite into the dense, chewy bar. It was sweet and stuck to her teeth, and it would provide the nutrients she'd need to keep her energy up.

The coyotes started up again, but they seemed to have moved farther away from them for the time being. Susanna finished the protein bar and tossed the wrapper into the storage box.

"We should try and get some sleep, too," Zeke said. "Can you sleep sitting up in that chair?"

"*Yah*, I think I can."

"You mind if I blow out the lamp?"

She actually found the light comforting, and the warmth from it felt nice, but she wouldn't sleep too well that way.

"Sure," she said. "That'll be fine."

Zeke blew out the flame, and for a moment, everything around her was pitch blackness. But then her eyes started to adjust and she saw the gray light from underneath the door and outside the windows, and Zeke's watch face had some little marks that glowed in the dark.

"Good night," Zeke said softly.

"Good night."

She tried to feel safer than she did. She tried to feel braver. But deep down, all she wanted was to be back in her community beside a potbellied stove with a pinging stovepipe and the soft sounds of people talking. She wanted to listen to the murmur of men talking about the weather, and the click-click-click of women's knitting needles.

Instead, she had the deep, even breathing from Zeke across from her. Was he sleeping already? Somehow she doubted it. But she shut her eyes all the same, and tried to think of cozier circumstances.

Zeke stretched his legs out. Sleeping in a camping chair wasn't going to be comfortable, but it was no worse than lying down on the floor would be.

Scanning the blind in the darkness, he could just barely make out Susanna's form in the darkness.

This was the first Amish woman Zeke had spoken to since he was a teenager who hadn't treated him like a different species. Rescuing her on the street probably had a lot to do with that. But when his parents left the faith, everything had changed. He was officially an outsider now. Amish folks were cautious around people who weren't Amish or who had jumped the fence. They were cautious around folks who were from a district with looser rules, too. So dressed like an Englisher and saying that his family had left the faith—that relegated him to the "unsafe" category.

But he'd felt like an outsider with the Englishers, too. He never quite understood their humor, and he didn't have the same childhood memories. He didn't watch TV growing up, hadn't gone to movies, hadn't played at arcades. None of it. And when he'd found a woman he thought he'd marry last year, he hadn't been good enough for her family, either. He felt like he was perpetually stuck on the outside of things—not Amish enough or English enough to really be accepted anywhere.

But that made him a good protector. You needed a night watchman—the kind of guy who could stay up while the rest were sleeping. You needed a sheepdog—someone willing to protect the flock while they grazed in peace. The people who never quite accepted him needed him more than they'd ever know. There were dangers out there that they didn't even think about because guys like him were chasing down the bad guys.

Outside, he heard the hoot of an owl, and he shut his eyes.

Gott, help me to protect this woman, he prayed. *And help me to figure out who's after her...*

Because he was absolutely certain that someone very dangerous had her in their crosshairs.

Zeke was starting to slip into sleep when he heard rustling and the snap of a twig somewhere outside. He lurched back into wakefulness, listening. A stick cracked, and farther off he heard voices.

"…out here somewhere."

"It's stupid dark out here. We aren't going to see anything."

"Shut up. There is only two of them, and someone had a fire out here. Ike said he saw the smoke, and the boss said they might be in these woods."

Zeke crept to the window and looked out. He could see the bob of two flashlights through the trees. They were coming in this direction, and if they got to the blind, he and Susanna would be fish in a barrel.

Coyotes howled again, and the sound of a gunshot silenced them. Susanna bolted upright.

"Shh," he whispered, putting a hand on her leg to reassure her. "We need to get out of here quietly. Okay? Are you awake?"

She slipped from her chair and it squeaked at her movement. How much could those men hear out there? He wasn't sure, but they had to move quickly. The sound of raucous laughter raised his hackles, but it gave him a sense of how far away the men were.

"We have to get out of here now," he whispered.

He pulled open the door and for a moment let his eyes adjust. It was dark out there, and the moon was behind a cloud—no help at all. The stairs creaked as he tried to tiptoe down them, and when he got to the bottom, he reached up and helped Susanna to jump down and avoid the stairs altogether. She landed in his arms with a little puff of exhaled air against his cheek.

"Check the blind," one man's voice said. "We'll circle around. I don't know what they think we'll find out here."

Another gunshot cracked through the air, and Zeke took the opportunity to run as the shot echoed, pulling Susanna with him.

"Cut it out!" one of the men said roughly. "Quit shooting at stuff, Arnie!"

Zeke and Susanna headed into the underbrush, a stick cracking loudly under his foot. He winced, and pulled Susanna behind a tree. All he could hear was his own breath and the thunder of his pulse in his ears.

"Did you here that?" a voice demanded. Zeke peeked around the tree. The men had emerged from the trees on the other side of the clearing. Three men were circling the blind now. One of them kicked at the ash and burned wood from their fire. Zeke pulled back behind the trunk, his mind spinning ahead. Did they need to go farther from the blind?

A coyote yipped and it sounded closer than he was entirely comfortable with, too.

God, where do we go? What direction is safe?

Right now he'd rather take his chances with wild animals than human beings, but he might change his mind about that right quick if he was facing down a pair of hungry coyotes or an angry black bear. He had a gun, but six bullets wouldn't take him far.

"Yeah, they were here," the man said, and he muttered an ugly oath. "It's still warm. Not too long ago."

"We'd have 'em if Arnie hadn't warned them off shooting at nothing," another male voice grumbled. "You're an idiot, Arnie."

Footsteps sounded on the wooden steps, and when Zeke

peeked around the tree again, he saw a man reemerge from the blind.

"They ate our food! And where's my picture of the hot chick?"

Right…he'd taken that down. Zeke didn't feel bad about that, either.

A flashlight beam hit the brush next to them, and Zeke held Susanna close, her thundering heartbeat reverberating against his chest.

"So they were out here," one of the men said. "We'll have to tell the boss he was right. Fan out. Let's see if we can find them."

Zeke looked around himself as he heard the men spread out, footsteps crunching through the brush.

"Come out, come out, wherever you are!" a man sang out in a creepy voice not too far away.

"Shut up, Arnie," one of the other men barked. "We don't get paid to be theatrical."

It was then that Zeke looked up—a desperate reaching of heart and mind toward his Maker—and as he looked, he saw the perfectly spaced tree limbs. That was the answer! They needed to get off the ground as high as possible.

He pointed upward, catching Susanna's gaze. She looked in the same direction, then nodded. Thank goodness she was Amish—she would have grown up climbing trees, and with a little blessing and some muscle memory, they could get up this one, too.

The men seemed to be thundering off in the other direction, but Zeke didn't trust that. Arnie's holloing was going that way at least, and his compatriots continued to tell him to hush.

Zeke cupped his hands to give Susanna a boost. She lifted one side of her skirt, put a foot in his palms, and he boosted her as high as he could. She caught one of the higher branches and pulled herself up. She was a quick climber, and made her way upward, staying close to the trunk. He caught the farthest limb he could reach and hoisted himself up into the trees.

This spruce was rough and sappy, but there was space enough to move upward. Susanna was above, and she'd stopped moving toward the top, the tree swaying in the night wind. Zeke went up another couple of branches and then stopped, too.

Beneath them, through the branches, he could make out the slice of flashlight beams beneath them.

They circled around, and then came in their direction, the men passing underneath the tree that held them. Zeke looked down on top of one dirty baseball cap, and held his breath.

"You see anything?" Another man materialized next to him.

"Nah."

"It's hard to see anything in this darkness." The flashlight dimmed. "Shoot." He shook it, and the dim light flickered. "It's out of battery."

"Yeah, we'd better head back. They aren't out here."

The men moved on, their footsteps quieter than the others, but still audible. The coyotes howled again, and the men picked up their pace.

"All right, they were definitely here, but they're gone now," the leader called. "We'll call it in. I don't see any sign of them now. They might have gone out to the road. That's what I would do. Fan out, and we'll cover as much ground as possible heading back toward the road."

The call of the coyotes made the leader look nervously over his shoulder.

The men headed away, back through the clearing, and he watched as their flashlight beams melted into the forest, their voices muffling, and then disappearing. The odd snap of a stick seemed to travel farther than the voices did.

"Let's stay here for a few more minutes," Zeke said softly. "Just in case they circle back around."

"*Yah.* Let's do that." Her voice was quiet, but it shook slightly. She was scared, and he didn't blame her.

For the next half hour they clung to their branches until his muscles started to ache from not moving. There was no sign of the men returning, but the coyotes were closer now, and they were sounding hungry.

He had to decide—where was safest now? In this tree? Or back in the blind where the coyotes couldn't get at them?

"What do you think?" he called softly upward.

Susanna looked down at him.

"Do you want to stay here until the sun comes up, or go back to the blind?"

"Are they coming back?"

"I doubt they'll come back tonight," he said. "I don't know about you, but my muscles are getting sore."

"Mine, too," she said.

A coyote yipped, and another answered. They were closer now. A few coyotes together set up a howl, and a shiver slid down his spine.

"I don't think we should be traveling on foot," he said. "There are hungry animals out here, and we're vulnerable."

The moon slid out from behind the cloud and the whole forest seemed to illuminate in its silvery glow. They might even stand out in this tree in full moonlight—Susanna's dress and apron would, at least.

"To the blind, then," she said. "Although I doubt I'll sleep much."

"Yeah, me, neither," he agreed. But the blind was their best option for the rest of the night.

He carefully climbed down and dropped to the pine needle–covered ground. Susanna was slower in her descent, but she made it down, too. He caught her as she dropped the last few feet.

He took one last look around and, seeing no sign of those men, they crept across the newly illumined clearing, and back into the blind. Zeke left the door open a little, though, so he could see outside.

"They saw our fire, didn't they?" she asked him.

"They did. No more boiling water now. We'll have to find water elsewhere."

She nodded.

"Try to sleep," he whispered.

"I don't think I can."

"Try. We'll be on our feet at first light."

Susanna sank into the camping chair, and Zeke leaned back into his. But he wasn't going to trust that darkness again. Those men knew where to look, and come daylight, he and Susanna had to be on the move before they came back.

Zeke didn't sleep well, as was to be expected in a camping chair. He woke up several times—once to a noise outside that turned out to be a solitary, prowling timber wolf. The next time he woke up, his watch said it was one in the morning, and his hips were sore from the position he was sleeping in. And the last time he awoke, it was from a dream about wolves nipping at his heels, and Amish girls who kept disappearing behind trees. He woke up in a cold sweat in the dim light of dawn.

Susanna was asleep, her head tipped to the side and her chest rising and falling with her deep, even breaths. At least she was getting some rest, but they needed to get out of here before anyone returned. Zeke had to make a plan. She looked rumpled, and her dress was dirty. Her white *kapp* was less than white now.

"Susanna," he whispered.

She startled awake.

"Good morning," he said softly.

"Morning…" She licked her lips and sat up, rubbing the back of her neck.

"We've got to move," he said, and he handed her one of the last protein bars. "Breakfast."

Susanna bowed her head in silence before tearing her protein bar open. Zeke silently thanked God for the food they'd found, but he didn't close his eyes. They headed out of the blind cautiously, and Zeke looked around. He had a prickling feeling like they were being watched, and he scanned the trees, looking for some unseen threat. In police training, they'd been told to never ignore that prickling feeling because some part of your subconscious was picking up on a threat that your conscious mind hadn't spotted yet.

But where? What was it? They'd heard the men approaching in the night. Were they coming more quietly this time?

Wind rustled through the trees, and somewhere close by a woodpecker was tapping on a tree. Something scurried through the underbrush. He looked around carefully, not seeing anything amiss.

"Is there any more food we can bring with us?" Susanna asked.

"No, this is it."

A protein bar each. It wasn't much, but it was better than nothing. God would need to provide for them—but they'd gotten this far. Maybe they could make it to a phone this morning and be in a nice safe police station with some fast food by noon. That was a cheering thought.

That prickling feeling on the back of his neck intensified, and then the sound of helicopter blades broke through the morning stillness. That was it! He must have been making out the sound of the helicopter's approach without realizing it. He felt a wave of satisfaction at having figured it out, but at the same time, they only had moments to spare. His self-congratulation could wait.

"Under the blind!" he ordered.

"What?" She looked over at him, stunned.

He wordlessly grabbed her hand and tugged her after him underneath the stilted structure. They couldn't stand upright, and he realized that their shadows stretched long in the early morning sunlight. They might be hidden under the blind from anyone looking down on them, but their shadows were not!

"Lie down," he said, and this time she seemed to understand his meaning more quickly, because she crouched down on the ground, and when he dropped to his belly, she spread out on the ground next to him.

Some small stones and a crunchy pine cone dug into his belly, but their shadows no longer showed them as people— just lumps. A moment later the helicopter came flying low over the forest. He squinted, trying to make out the type of helicopter it was. It wasn't the green and white of Life Flight or the black and white of state police. It was a rusty orange color, and whoever was flying was looking for something— or someone. That was no rescue helicopter—it was private.

"Who is it?" she breathed.

"I can't tell," he replied. "Don't move."

The helicopter circled around, coming lower, and Zeke's mind started to race ahead. What direction did they run if the chopper tried to land in the clearing? Right now, they weren't visible from above—nothing more than their shadows, which hopefully didn't betray that they were people. The beating blades whomped against the air as the helicopter dipped lower, then pulled back up again.

Did the pilot suspect something? Were they coming down?

But then the door on the side of the helicopter opened, and Zeke saw a man with a large gun—he couldn't make out more than that before gunshots rang through the air and bullets splintered the hunting blind one after the other. If they'd been inside it they'd be dead, he realized in one sickening moment.

But they weren't inside.

His mind was jumping ahead now. They'd certainly be killed if they stayed, and they were in God's hands alone if they ran. He'd take his chances with God's hands covering them. Then the chopper passed, moving from directly above them to do another circle.

"Run!" he snapped and, grabbing Susanna's arm, he lurched to his feet.

There was a stand of dense trees just behind them—in the same direction the men had disappeared last night, and he pulled her in that direction. They'd mentioned a road— maybe they could get to it.

They plunged into the clinging underbrush and forged ahead. His heart was beating in time with those thumping blades, and while Susanna was slower than he was, he didn't loosen his grip on her.

"Keep running!" he shouted between ragged breaths.

Overhead, he could hear the helicopter circling, looking for signs of them. All he could do now was pray that God kept them hidden from sight as they plunged deeper into the forest. The more dense the canopy, the better concealed they would be. But Susanna was wearing bright blue and white—she'd stand out.

Zeke ran until his lungs were on fire and his feet felt like lead, and he was mostly carrying Susanna as she stumbled along behind him. Then he stopped against the thick trunk of a dense tree, and pulled Susanna with him against it, both of them breathing hard. At least they wouldn't be seen from overhead.

"The helicopter is landing by the blind," Zeke said, his breath coming in heaves. "They're checking if we were inside—if we're dead…"

"Who are they?" Susanna wheezed. She leaned over, her hands on her knees.

"I have no idea, but they're pulling in all of their resources," he said.

"For me…"

He didn't answer. But yes, it was all for her. Why this one Amish woman? What did they think she knew?

"They must have figured we'd come back, and they came in the first light of day when they could see something," he said.

It was smart. It was what he'd do if he were in their shoes. They'd seen the smoke; they knew that he and Susanna had been there. They also probably could appreciate how hungry and tired they were. They were running on fumes, and their pursuers knew it. He felt like a cornered rabbit—and those men were stronger. Organized. Bloodthirsty.

Susanna's shoulders started to shake, and her already ragged breathing became shorter and panicked. Her wide eyes met his, her lips pale and her hands trembling. This was shock. So he did the only thing he could think of to calm her down. He pulled her into his arms and pressed her against his chest. He calmed his own breath, making each inhale and exhale slow and deep.

She was shaking, so he smoothed a hand over her hair. Her *kapp*, which had survived their dash, was hanging by one pin, and he plucked it off her head and leaned his cheek against her warm hair. She clutched his shirt in her fists at his sides, but her trembling stopped.

"We'll be okay," he murmured. "I've got a plan."

It was a very loose plan at this point. Mostly it consisted of keeping her alive until he could get to a telephone and contact the Pennsylvania State Police. But he suddenly realized with absolute certainty that he *would* keep her alive, even if it meant absorbing bullets for her.

"They want to kill me…" she said, and she lifted her head up. "Zeke, they really want to kill me!"

"They probably want a lot of things," he said. "Doesn't mean they're going to get it. And don't feel too special. They'd gladly kill me, too, I'm sure."

She blinked at him.

"That was a bit of a joke," he said. He released his tight grip on her, but he kept his hands on her shoulders as she straightened.

"You okay now?" he asked.

"As okay as I'll get, I suppose," she said.

"Good." He looked in the direction of the helicopter landing somewhere in the vicinity of the blind. "I don't want to give them a chance to find us standing here. Let's keep moving." He squinted, looking up at the sky. "That way is west. We'll hit farmland eventually if we keep going that way. The men last night mentioned a road, too."

"What's the plan?" she asked.

"Walk west."

"And then?"

"And then we find a phone hut or somewhere with a telephone. Maybe a barn. Maybe a phone shanty. And I call in for backup."

"Okay."

He handed her the tattered *kapp*. It was gauzy material to begin with, and it was torn now. She touched her bare hair, and some color tinged her cheeks. For her, it was a form of modesty, and she'd never uncover her hair around a man. He averted his gaze, and when he looked back, she'd found the pins in her hair and had secured the tattered hair covering in place once more.

"Let's keep moving," he said.

He looked over his shoulder again. He could still hear those chopper blades through the trees, drowning everything else out. They needed to get out of here, and as far from those searching men as possible.

FIVE

It was another hour of trudging through the forest, winding around trees and being scratched by brambles and twigs. Susanna kept thinking she heard something behind her, only to turn and see nothing but trees, a cloud of mosquitoes or that faint green glow of sunlight trying to batter its way through a thick canopy of trees. If these men got her address off of a letter that was supposed to be sent to her from Hannah, then these were people connected to her cousin. Who else should be worried for their lives right now? Hannah's parents? But she hadn't been writing to them—not that they admitted to, at least. Hannah's parents had been attempting to use some tough love to get her to see reason. Now they'd likely never forgive themselves.

And then there was Shawn—the Englisher who loved her. What had happened to him? Somehow he felt like family, a little bit. He'd loved Hannah so much, and while he had taken her from her family—which was heartbreaking and as close to unforgivable as was possible for the Amish—he *had* loved her. Was Shawn okay? Had he gotten killed, too?

Bright sunlight sparkled through the trees, and then suddenly, they burst out onto a field. A smattering of cattle were grazing far off next to the crest of a hill, and the soft lowing of a cow calling her calf was carried on the grass-scented breeze toward them. A moldering barn stood about a hundred yards off, looking like an old man hunched under a great burden. She stood in the underbrush as Zeke looked around them, then up at the sky, squinting in the sunlight and shading his eyes. The peaceful field felt anything but with killers on their trail.

"Do you hear the helicopter?" he asked.

She listened, then shook her head. "No, not anymore."

"Thank God," he breathed. "This was the direction the men took when they left last night, I think. I don't see a road."

"Me, neither," she agreed.

Zeke chewed the side of his cheek, seeming undecided about their next step.

"I've been thinking about Shawn," she said. "If these people will go to these lengths to find me, what about Hannah's boyfriend? He was closer to her than I was."

Zeke nodded. "I still can't piece it together. What would they hope to gain by using all of this manpower, and all of these resources to chase down someone close to a girl they killed and dumped?"

"Who was Hannah to them?" Susanna asked.

He shook his head slowly. "I wish we knew." He sucked in a breath through his nose, then sighed. "We'd better find water. Maybe that barn will be close to something newer, and we can get to a hose or pump or something."

He started out into the field, stepping high over some grass-covered logs. He held out his hand to help her over one, and she took it, landing at his side, but then released it again. Susanna couldn't help but look over her shoulder as they headed in the direction of that sagging structure.

"We'll get into that old barn," Zeke said. "Then no one will be able to see us from above."

Susanna lengthened her stride as they hurried over the undulating grassland. Zeke held a hand out again, and for a moment she hesitated—it was not the Amish way—but she was tired and he was stronger, so she reached out and his fingers closed around hers. It was like being swept along in his wake, and she was suddenly so grateful for him that she had to blink back tears.

"You okay?" he asked, glancing over at her.

She nodded, not trusting herself to speak, and he slowed his pace just a little and tugged her in closer against his side. It felt so nice…except a thought suddenly occurred to her.

"Is there a woman who wouldn't like you holding my hand this way?" she blurted out. Was she holding the hand of another woman's man?

"No," he said. "I'm very single."

"Okay…good." He was single. It didn't matter in the grand scheme of things because he wasn't Amish, but she still didn't want to be crossing any lines she ought not to with another woman's fella. She wasn't that kind of woman, even in confusing and terrifying times.

"How about you?" he asked. "Do you have someone who'd take me to task for this?"

She smiled then. "My uncle might, or my Amish brothers. But don't worry about them."

Zeke laughed softly, then paused, looking up into the sky again and then all around them.

"I keep thinking I hear that helicopter," he said.

They picked up their pace again and Susanna was breathing hard by the time they reached the old barn. Zeke put a hand out to keep her from following him as he looked around the side of it.

"There's a house and a newer barn down that way," he

said, pointing to the right. "But let's be on the safe side and not let anyone see us just yet."

Zeke opened the barn door—it was ajar on rusted hinges—and they squeezed inside. The roof was sagging dangerously on one side, daylight shining through where entire patches of the roof were missing. But the other side looked secure enough. Some moldering bales were piled under a dry patch of roof, and the floor looked to be dirt. It was a pole barn—no foundation. Given enough time, the old barn would eventually crumple into a heap and get covered by grass. Nature was stronger than any man-made structure.

"Why?" Zeke asked, turning toward her.

"Why what?" she asked.

"Why were you asking if I was taken?"

"Because if you were, and I was holding your hand, it would be wrong," she said. And what it made her feel would be even worse, but she wasn't going to say that.

"Ah." He smiled faintly. "Right now, your bigger concern should be staying alive."

"It is, trust me." She eyed him for a moment. "Why aren't you with someone?"

Zeke was tall, strong, confident, handsome. If he were an Amish farmer, he'd have girls lining up at his door with their best baking in hand.

Zeke looked out the door again, then back at her. "Because I'm too different."

"Than the Englishers?" she asked.

"Being raised Amish changes a lot," he said.

She tried to wrap her mind around that, and Zeke pulled the barn door closed.

"But I can't blame my Amish upbringing entirely," he added. "I'm just that kind of guy who doesn't fit in. I'm more comfortable taking care of things on the periphery."

"So you've never had a girlfriend?" she asked.

"I was engaged up until last year," he said.

The faint sound of helicopter blades interrupted the stillness, and they both froze. The sound came closer, and then it seemed to start retreating again.

"Stay in the shadows," Zeke said, and they both pressed back, away from the gaping part of the roof. The sound grew quieter and then faded away again, and Susanna exhaled a sigh of relief.

"We should stay here a bit, just in case they come back," Zeke said. "We're sheltered here, at least."

Susanna nodded, and she upended two wooden crates. A mouse skittered out of one of them and disappeared into the shadows. She didn't startle, though, and they both sat down. For a moment, they sat in silence, listening to the ever-fading chopper sound.

"Are we safe?" she whispered.

"I'm not sure." The Pennsylvania Dutch accent was a little stronger again. "For now, I suppose we are. If we stay put for a bit. I keep thinking about last night. Those men claimed that the contents of the blind belonged to them. So they're local."

"From here?" she asked.

"Maybe." He licked his lips. "Are you thirsty?"

She nodded.

"We'll give it a few minutes, and then I'll go see if I can find us some water," he said. "But together, we stand out. Especially you in your dirty dress. So you'll stay here while I go investigate where we are. From overhead, if I'm by myself I might just look like a local farmer."

They fell into silence again, and Susanna looked over at Zeke. When she first saw him, he looked so foreign—the clothes, the gun, the steely look in his eyes. But now that she'd spent more time with him, he seemed more like regular Amish men with a tender core underneath the trappings.

"So what happened?" she asked softly. "To your engagement?" He didn't look inclined to answer, so she added, "If you tell me about yours, I'll tell you about mine."

Zeke looked over at her then. "You were engaged?"

"You first." She gave him the same mischievous smile she used to give her older brothers.

Susanna saw something almost boyish glitter in his eyes.

"Fine. Me, first. Kinsey and I dated for about a year. I proposed, she said yes, and her family wasn't really keen on that. I wasn't educated enough for them. Her dad was a lawyer. Her mom was a doctor. They were…a cut above the likes of me."

A lawyer, a doctor, a police detective… They all seemed pretty similar to her. What was the difference?

"But you help people, too," she said.

"*Yah*, but I don't make much money doing it. We cops aren't highly paid civil servants."

Right. The income. At least in an Old Order Amish community, money was seen as a necessary tool, not a status symbol.

"And this mattered to Kinsey?" she asked.

"Her parents' approval did. We ended up breaking up over it. It was just a big strain on our relationship."

"Hmm." She nodded. So that explained him—the not-Amish-enough man who wasn't rich enough for the girl he'd loved, either. "I'm sorry that happened."

"*Danke*," he replied. "Now you. What happened to your engagement?"

The Pennsylvania Dutch was slipping back into his language again, she noticed.

"We were writing letters. He was from another community, and we'd visited each other a couple of times," she replied. "This was before my *daet* died. Anyway, he'd asked me to marry him, and then one day I got a letter, and he'd called it off."

"No face-to-face explanation?"

She shook her head. "He married another girl the next fall."

"Was he cheating?"

"I doubt it. I think he just…knew what he wanted when he saw it." And ultimately, it hadn't been Susanna. He now had two little *kinner* with his wife. And last Susanna had heard through a mutual friend, his wife was pregnant with their third. That breakup had been embarrassing and painful, and she'd stopped trying after that. So maybe she understood Zeke a little bit.

"I thought it would be easier in an Amish community," he said. "At least everyone wants the same thing—marriage and kids."

"Didn't Kinsey want those things?" she asked.

"I guess it's more complicated still," he replied. "Because she did want those things. I guess I just didn't tick all the boxes for her."

He hadn't been good enough—she didn't like that. He was a good man, and a good woman should recognize that, and be grateful for it.

"Well, even with every man wanting a wife and *kinner* out here in Amish country, I still ended up an old maid. These things happen."

"How old are you?" he asked, squinting.

"Twenty-seven."

"Ancient." He chuckled, and his laughter stung. She knew her situation, and it wasn't a laughing matter to her. Women her age had several *kinner* already. And the men who were looking to get married were several years younger than she was now.

"Sorry. Susanna, the joke here is that you are actually not ancient. Out there—in the rest of the country—twenty-seven is still considered pretty young."

"Oh…" So maybe his laughter hadn't meant what she'd thought.

He leaned over and nudged her arm with his. "Out there in regular America, you're just a young woman putting her life together. It's all in the perspective."

"And what are you out there?" she asked.

"Jaded." He smiled, though, taking the edge off the word.

He pushed himself to his feet then and went back to the door. He listened for a moment, and then pushed it open. He looked around, disappeared outside for a moment, and then returned.

"Okay," he said. "I'm going to find us some water. You stay here, and wait for me. If anyone comes before I get back—"

"Hide," she said.

"Yah." He met her gaze with a warmth that almost looked tender. "Hold on."

He pulled the gun out of his holster and put it into her hands. She recoiled.

"Just for safety until I get back," he said. "Susanna, this is important so listen. Now, this pistol is a Walther PDP, and it doesn't have a safety for you to release before you can shoot. You just have to pull the trigger back all the way. Have you ever shot a gun before?"

"No, and I can't kill someone," she said, her voice shaking

"Then don't kill them. Just…stop them."

She looked down at the heavy black pistol in her hand.

Guns had one purpose—killing. Sometimes they were made to kill animals for food, but not this one.

Gott, don't let anyone get close enough to make me use this! she prayed.

"Now, you wait here," Zeke said. "I won't be too long."

He disappeared again out the door, and she put the gun aside on an old, grayed bale of hay. She didn't want to touch it. She crept forward into the patch of sunlight where the roof was broken, and she looked out a crack in the barn wall. Zeke walked casually enough through the shin-length grass. He walked like he belonged there, like he was just a man out there inspecting his own field.

She licked her lips. Her mouth was feeling sticky now, and she was thinking longingly of that pot of boiled water back at the hunting blind.

The blind seemed to belong to the men who were after her. She remembered that picture on the wall of the scantily clad woman holding a gun. She shivered. Was that considered ordinary for Englishers or for nonbelievers? What did they want out of women? It seemed so demeaning. A woman was sometimes a wife, sometimes a mother, but always a guardian of the home and of the community, whether she was married or not. A woman was a treasure to her community and to her Gott. But there was something about that casual display of skin in that picture on the wall in the hunting shack, the casual holding of a gun, that made her wonder if the people in these parts would have any of the Christian charity that she and Zeke needed so desperately.

Oh, Gott...help us!

Zeke headed through the field up to the crest of the hill. He wanted to look like he belonged if anyone flew over above. They'd be looking for a man and woman together, not just a man checking his pasture, so he hoped the ruse would work. But he didn't want to just walk up to whatever house was waiting over that hill considering just how close those men had been last night. He had a feeling they were local—maybe not on this farm, but somewhere close by. So he ambled over toward a copse of trees to shelter him while he made a plan.

He looked over his shoulder at the dilapidated barn. It looked innocent enough, but it was the obvious hiding spot in this area. If anyone caught him, they'd know exactly where to look for Susanna, and that was worrisome.

She was an interesting combination of sweet and strong. That was a combination that came with Amish girls, from what he could remember. They could start a fire in a stove, cook for a crowd, organize a household, milk a cow…and then the image of Susanna's tear-filled eyes looking up at him nearly broke him in two. Susanna was tough enough, but six bullets wouldn't get her far. If she even pulled the trigger, which he wasn't sure she'd even do. The Amish were pacifists.

Amish men knew their jobs—and ironically enough, that Amish instinct had led Zeke to law enforcement. The Amish man's duty was to protect the strong, devoted woman who relied upon him, and Zeke's Amish instincts were melding with his training right now. It wasn't just his job to protect her. It was starting to feel like a heart-level necessity, and that wasn't good. He needed some emotional distance if he was going to keep ahead of these people.

Zeke crested the hill beside the little copse of trees, and he ducked down and surveyed the farm below. This was an English farm with tractors and a pickup truck. But there were more people there than seemed normal, which made him pretty certain these were the same people who'd come after them last night. There were several rows of green-houses, and there were two large rottweilers chained up—nothing ordinary about that. One of the men tossed each of them a big, fresh beef bone.

Zeke looked back toward the old barn. Should they move on now? The detective in him wanted to get closer and check things out, but he was unarmed and outnumbered. Still, he was torn for a moment until he spotted some plastic-covered flats of bottled water behind a separate garage. There were a few stray bottles sitting next to the pile of flats, and he swallowed hard... Water. His mouth was already sticky with thirst, and Susanna was thirsty, too.

Clouds scudded in front of the sun, and Zeke waited until the men started toward the house, and then he cautiously made his way down the embankment toward the farm. He got as far as a barbed wire fence, and he rolled into the ditch right before it, waiting breathlessly for a moment. When he heard no noise, he peeked up and found that the men were heading inside, and the dogs were lying down now, their teeth grinding against their bones.

The dogs were occupied. Thank God for that! There was a big metal feeder with a round bale inside near the fence, and Zeke said a silent prayer and then kept low and dashed behind the feeder. Still no alarm from the dogs.

The greenhouses were just beyond, and Zeke eyed the closest one, which was a good hundred yards from the dogs. He was familiar with that type of greenhouse. They came in prefabricated packs, and they had back doors to them, too.

The greenhouses could be used for anything—drugs, girls... The criminals working here were obviously an organized group, and that normally meant they'd be dabbling in all the regular moneymaking schemes: drugs, gambling and prostitution. Prostitution didn't always point to human trafficking, but it normally did. He'd take the opportunity to peek in those greenhouses, grab some water, and then he'd get back to Susanna and they'd keep moving.

Zeke moved as quietly as possible as he slipped behind the first greenhouse. The back door was locked from the outside—weird. He peeked into a window. There were some plants that looked like marijuana, and he saw some boxes piled up, some brown paper packages on a table… Yeah, that all looked suspiciously like drugs. But still, an outside-facing lock felt odd for a back door, even if the greenhouses were being used for storage of valuable drug hauls. But the dogs were chained in front of the next greenhouse. If they weren't guarding this haul, what was in the other one?

He crept toward the next greenhouse, the grass muffling the sounds of his movements. The windows had been covered for this building, though, and he found one window in the back where the cloth cover had fluttered loose in one corner, and he could just peek inside.

This one had no plants inside, but there were some boxes, a few crates, and in the muted light of one corner near the front of the building, he saw a pile of blankets and what looked like a running shoe.

His heart slammed to a stop when his eyes adjusted and he could make out the prone figure of a girl in a purple floral-patterned dress. Her hands were bound, and she looked to be unconscious. She had no *kapp* on her head, but her long hair was pulled back into a bun that was coming loose, and a kerchief lay close by as if it had fallen off her hair. She didn't look Amish, but she had the look of some of the more conservative Weaverland Mennonites in the area. She looked young—couldn't be more than eighteen. She was slim, and she reminded him of his own sister at that age so strongly that he had to hold himself back from pounding through the door then and there. But he had no backup, and there were a lot of armed men on this farm who would kill him, Susanna and this poor girl.

He slammed a wall up between himself and his emotions.

Gott, show me what to do!

A table was across the building from her, and he could see some articles on the tabletop that looked like syringes. Was she drugged, then? He looked back at the girl. She wasn't moving, and the position she was lying in looked uncomfortable. So yes, his guess was that she was drugged. It was an easy way to keep a kidnap victim silent and under control.

Could he get in there? He slowly tried the locked back door—there was no getting through. Plus, they'd probably have some alarms in place to warn them if any doors opened that shouldn't be opening. They were cheap enough to buy at any electronics store these days.

He looked back toward the field—it was a fair distance to go carrying an unconscious girl. She wasn't petite, either. She looked like she was on the tall side, so that would make her considerably heavier. If she were awake, it would be a different story.

Gott, I can't just leave her here!

But the likelihood of him getting her out without anyone seeing them was slim to none. What he needed was backup. He needed other troopers, fully armed, and their own K9 officers to boot. This place was well guarded.

He looked in the window again. The girl hadn't moved, but he saw her hand twitch. So she was definitely alive.

Footsteps crunched over the gravel, coming in his direction, and Zeke held his breath. There was the sound of a lock opening. The dogs jumped up and started to bark and whine.

"Killer, sit." An order for the dog.

"So where are they sending her?" The other voice sounded just a little bit hesitant. Maybe he was a new recruit and the actual work was hard for him to stomach yet.

"I don't know. Does it matter?"

"I guess not. What's our quota?"

"Daniel Schaber says we need three. Her and two more." A pause. "Killer! Sit!" He cursed. "Unchain the dogs."

Zeke's heart hammered hard in his chest. The dogs were about to be loose, and they were moving the girl into the house. He'd seen at least six armed men go inside. And they weren't even pausing in their kidnapping efforts—two more girls were going to be targeted, and then only God knew what it would take to get them back again.

"Schaber says to bring her into the house for now. They have to wake her up, clean her up and make her a little more presentable." The door opened and Zeke crouched down, freezing in place. He worked his fingers and toes, keeping himself in touch with his body, with his surroundings.

Daniel Schaber must be their boss—at least locally. And he was in that house, by the sounds of it. The name didn't ring any immediate bells, but Zeke's fingers were itching to check a few databases. If only he had his cell phone.

"What did he say about the other girl?"

"The chick who didn't die in the burned-out car?"

"That's the one."

"All he said was that they're in the woods," one man was saying. "We'll get some supplies and a team of us will fan out through the forest. They might be in the forest still, or they might have hit the road. We have patrols looking on all the roads right now, and I'll take a team into the forest to be thorough."

"They should be easy enough to catch."

They were going to head for the forest—right past that

old barn! Could he distract them? Or maybe he could get back fast enough to move Susanna out of reach before they got moving.

"I can't believe that chick isn't dead yet."

"I know. We'll get her. What's Schaber's preoccupation with her, anyway?"

"No idea. But he wants her in his hands, alive or dead. There were no human remains in the burned-out car, and he says they saw two people in the hunting blind when they flew over, so it's a pretty good chance it's them."

"So shoot on sight?"

"Those are our orders."

There was some rustling, a thump, a few grunts, and then the man who seemed to be the leader of the two ordered the other to lock the door.

When Zeke peeked into the building, the girl was gone, her kerchief lying on the greenhouse floor. When he looked around the building, he saw the men striding away, the girl flung over the bigger man's shoulder like a bag of flour. He could see a nasty scrape on the side of her face from here.

He'd left his gun with Susanna… But even if he hadn't, Zeke had no access to police backup, and was one man against an army. Plus, Susanna was waiting for him, and he had to get her out of here, too. But watching them walk away, he felt like he was going to vomit.

Gott, I'm one man! Protect that girl, and help us to get to her. Please—put Your hand over her and let us get her back!

The men tramped up the steps to the house and disappeared inside. God willing, Zeke was coming back for that girl, too. With backup. And these men were going to pay on this side of glory.

SIX

This barn felt like it held some sort of sordid history—the kind that made people abandon it completely to rot into the ground. Susanna looked cautiously around herself. It felt different in here alone, her only company that of a pistol lying on a bale of hay. There had been stalls on the far side of the barn where the roof had caved in. Some rusted horseshoes were scattered across the dirt floor. Forgotten. No longer needed.

The Amish didn't abandon their buildings. They fixed them again and again, pulling together as a community and repairing what might otherwise be lost. They gave new purpose to old timbers, and built upon their history.

The English abandoned and moved on.

But then…so had her siblings. Maybe she could halfway understand the ones who went English, but not the sister and brother who had stayed Amish. They'd walked away from their home community, from their ailing father, from her. And they'd simply left Susanna behind, moving on to brighter futures and new families. They got married, had *kinner*, developed strong ties to their in-laws. And all the while, they had a sister back at home who'd needed support, and she hadn't gotten any. No one had come to see what she needed. No one had even thought of helping her to find a husband! And here she was running for her life, and it was an ex-Amish cop who was stepping in. What had become of her that Zeke was all she had left?

Susanna looked up at the empty hole where the roof had caved in. Dark clouds scudded in front of the sun now. They were the kind of clouds that could threaten and do nothing... or unleash a torrent.

If Susanna's siblings had stayed, she wouldn't have been living alone. She would have had her brothers, sisters-in-law, her sisters... She would have had family here with her—more than just her aunt and uncle and Hannah. They would have pulled together and made a plan. But they hadn't stayed, and not one of them had worried about Susanna, either. She'd been their solution for their ailing father, and that was where their worries stopped.

And she was resentful about that. The youngest daughter who'd been left behind in every way possible. What about *her* future?

Susanna crept forward and looked through the crack in the wall. She couldn't see Zeke through her narrow vantage point, and she sent up a prayer for his safety. Maybe he was finding some friendly people who'd help. That was a possibility, wasn't it?

She moved away from the wall, listening for the sound of the chopper again. Did she hear it far off? It was hard to tell. She was listening so hard that she could very well be imagining it at this point.

What kind of people came with a helicopter and guns? People who killed, obviously.

Susanna heard the creak of the barn door hinges. She'd missed someone's approach, and her heart skipped a fearful beat. She slid behind the moldering bales of hay, her nose tickling with the dust. Only then did she spot the gun lying in full view, but she didn't dare grab it now. She felt like her own thundering heartbeat might give her away. She covered her nose and mouth with one hand, stifling a sneeze, and she blinked furiously against the urge.

"Susanna?" Zeke whispered.

She exhaled a relieved sigh, and crawled out of her hiding spot. Zeke's face was ashen, but he held two bottles of water and handed one over to her mutely. She grabbed the bottle, cracked it open and took a long drink.

"We need to get out of here," Zeke whispered as she swallowed gulp after gulp of sweet water. "And quietly. Whoever is after you has men stationed at that farm. They know it was us in the forest, and they think we might still be in the trees. They're sending a team out to find us in the woods, and they have patrols on the roads."

She drained the last of the water and her pulse started to pound as she tried to sort through this new information.

"What do we do?" she asked breathlessly.

"We stay away from the trees for now," he said, and he pressed his lips together. "Susanna, I'm going to be honest. None of it looks good. I say we go for the road. Sure they'll have patrols, but they can't cover every mile all the time. There's going to be a phone shanty somewhere. We have to call for help, or flag down a passing vehicle."

"Can we stay here for a bit?" she asked. "Can we just hide out? I can show you the spot I found."

"They have dogs."

Her breath seeped out of her lungs. Dogs would be able to sniff them out.

"I didn't want to freak you out," Zeke said softly and he eased back to look out the door, then turned his attention back to her, "but they've got another girl that they've kidnapped. I saw her. She looks like Weaverland Mennonite.

They're not moving her quite yet, but they will transfer her somewhere else, that's a guarantee."

Another girl! Her head started to spin. They weren't stopping!

He scrubbed a hand through his hair. "I couldn't get to her, and she's unconscious right now. They've moved her into the house—where there is a lot more security. If she has any hope of rescue, we need to call for police backup."

Another girl taken, another girl suffering, and a family panicking. And maybe another girl dead if they weren't fast enough.

"Is there any way we can get to her on our own and get her out of there?" she asked.

"Susanna, if there were, I'd already have done it. I didn't want to leave her there, but there was no way to get into that house without the cavalry. There are too many of them, and they're armed." He opened his water bottle and drained it. "And they are definitely looking for you. They mentioned you specifically—from the burned-out car and from the hunting blind. We need to get you out of here."

Zeke took her water bottle, and he stashed both bottles under some hay, and then he turned for the door and peeked out once more. Then he froze.

"Get back!"

Susanna froze, and Zeke pushed her toward her hiding spot. Her legs suddenly started to move of their own volition and she squatted down behind those dusty bales, and Zeke slipped in next to her. Far off, she heard the sound of men's voices, then the deep bark of a dog. She held her breath, her heart suspended in prayer for their protection. Something small—a rat maybe?—nibbled audibly on something close by.

Zeke caught her hand in his firm, dry grip and she slid a

hand over his forearm—somehow feeling stronger for the contact. The voices grew nearer, and then they seemed to pass by and continue on. She started to move, but Zeke's grip on her hand grew so strong that it started to hurt her fingers—she got the message. She stilled, willing her cramped legs to relax.

Something rattled against the door, and the hinges squeaked. Someone was coming inside to check. In response, Susanna heard the scratch of feet erupt over the floor, and she just made out the black-and-white tail of a skunk. A male voice cursed, and retreated. It didn't sound like the door had shut, though.

Thank Gott for that skunk to chase the man off!

After what felt like an eternity, Zeke released her hand and eased away from her and walked out from their hiding place. He picked up his gun and holstered it. The skunk was gone—probably escaped outside through a hole or crack in the wall.

"Okay," he whispered, and Susanna crawled out after him, her legs shaking from the fear and the cramped position. He held out a hand and she took it, letting him pull her to her feet.

"They're going for the forest," he whispered. "As soon as they go into the trees, we're heading across the field as fast as we can run. You see those cows over there?"

He pointed out the door, and she leaned to look. The cattle were scattered across the field, some standing, others lying down.

"Yah."

"We will dive behind them. Look to make sure everything is still clear, and then we run for those far trees. They aren't forest, they just separate us from the road. Got it?"

She nodded again.

Zeke bowed his head. "*Herr Gott*, protect us. Shield us. Put Your hand over us. In Jesus's name."

"Amen," she whispered. The prayer had calmed that fluttering in her chest, and it was like she could feel Gott's presence coming in close and protective.

"Now, we run."

Zeke eased sideways out the still-open barn door, and Susanna followed his lead. The men had disappeared into the woods, but the dog could still be heard, a deep bark echoing back toward them. Zeke grabbed her hand, and Susanna hoisted her skirt with her free hand, and they ran.

Susanna let her legs stretch out into a fast sprint, just managing to keep up with Zeke. The cows looked up in surprise, one lurching to her feet, as Zeke dove behind the large animal. Susanna followed him, landing next to him in the lush, fragrant grass. Overhead the clouds were growing denser, and the smell of rain lingered in the air, although not a drop had fallen yet.

Zeke slowly raised his head, and then crouched back again.

"Wait," he whispered.

"Killer!" A man's voice echoed from the tree line. "Get back over here, you lazy mutt! This way!"

The dog had sensed them. Susanna's throat closed off with fear, and she waited. Would this "killer" come sniffing them out?

"Killer!" the man shouted. "Come! Now!"

They waited in silence, the only sound Susanna could hear was her own thundering heartbeat and the grinding of the cow's teeth as she chewed her cud. The man's voice started moving away again and, after a moment, Zeke raised his head again.

"Okay. Let's run!"

Susanna pushed herself to her feet again, and she followed

Zeke in a dash toward a barbed wire fence, just before the trees. Barbed wire! Only now did it register that they'd have to get over it. Zeke got there first and pulled the wire down. She hoisted her skirt, but she couldn't get her leg up over it.

"Hold on." Zeke slammed his foot down on the wire and a staple popped from the post, finally giving her the space she needed to jump over the rusted barbs. Zeke followed her, and they pushed into the trees.

A mist of rain started to fall, filtering down through the leaves overhead. A vehicle passed on the road, and she saw red paint as it zipped past. They were very close by the road now, and they paused, breathing hard.

"We have to get away from this property," Zeke whispered. "Come on—"

Susanna reached out and caught his hand, hurrying to keep up with his longer stride. They clambered up the side of the ditch to the road, and they ran across the street and down into the ditch beyond.

"Okay, let's keep moving away from the forest," Zeke said. "We need to put distance between ourselves and those men looking for us."

Susanna didn't need to be told twice, and they headed in the opposite direction as the rain started to fall in earnest.

"Is this rain a good thing?" she asked softly as they hurried along together. "I mean for the dogs tracking us—will it help to wash away our scent?"

"I wish it were," he replied, his voice low. He slowed, the sound of a dog barking in the distance. "Rain actually enhances scent for the dogs. But we have one thing in our favor."

"What's that?" Susanna could use some good news about now.

"They've got rottweilers, not bloodhounds. Their dogs are better guard dogs than sniffer dogs."

It was something, but the sound of those dogs' deep barks out there in the trees made the hair on the back of her neck stand up.

Then in the distance, she spotted a vehicle coming slowly down the road. Zeke pulled her farther into the ditch and she squinted, trying to see through the drizzle.

"Can we flag them down for help?" she whispered.

"Wait…"

And then the vehicle came into view.

A blue van.

Zeke pulled Susanna back down into the ditch. The van was moving slowly—no doubt this was one of the promised patrols. But he still felt safer nearer the roads than in that forest right now. This just felt right, on a gut level. He tended to attribute those strong feelings to God's guidance.

He grabbed Susanna's arm, and pointed up from the ditch and into the trees at the side of the road. She nodded, turning wide, terrified eyes to him. And in that moment, all he wanted to do was make it better, to pull her into his arms, to tell her it would be okay. He wanted to be her problem solver, her hero, but there wasn't time for any of that.

He looked back again at the approaching van, his pulse speeding up, and his training slamming on top of it. He needed to get Susanna out of here. She was the one they were after, and he knew in that moment that he was willing to sacrifice himself to get her free.

As if in response to his own rising courage, a gust of wind whipped the rain sideways. Rain might help sniffer dogs, but it was terrible for visibility. Grabbing Susanna's arm, they scrambled up the bank and then dove into the trees. The underbrush snagged at his pants and shoelaces, and he could see that it was slowing Susanna down, tearing at her skirt. He needed that dirty blue skirt out of sight—now! So he hooked an arm around her waist and pulled her back behind a wide tree trunk. He lowered her to the ground and put a warning finger on his lips.

Had they been fast enough? He could only hope the blowing rain might have been enough to blur the vision of the men in the truck.

Sending up a silent prayer, he peeked around the far side of the tree. The blue van approached at the same pace, and he could see someone looking out an open window, peering into the brush on their side of the road. He pulled back.

Susanna was perfectly still except for the rapid rise and fall of her chest, but she didn't look scared like she had before. Now she looked…prepared. Like she was ready to fight for her life.

Good—that was better than terrified and trembling. They'd get through this, and he'd get her out of this somehow.

He could hear the van's engine as it drove past. It hadn't slowed, and he didn't dare look out from behind the tree again until it had gone past and all that was visible were red taillights.

"They're past," he whispered, and he held out a hand. Susanna accepted it and he helped her to her feet. But somehow, they were much closer to each other than he'd expected, and as she stood up, her foot caught on a root and her eyes widened as she stumbled backward. His first instinct was to reach out and grasp her to keep her upright, which left him nose to nose with her, his arm around her slim waist and her breath tickling his chin. There was a smudge of dirt on one cheek, and her *kapp* held on by a thread.

Suddenly, she wasn't the civilian he was trying to protect. She wasn't the target of a gang looking to kill her.

She was a beautiful woman who had the spirit of a warrior deep inside of her, and he'd never admired anyone so much in his entire life.

He looked down at her parted lips, and she put her hands on his chest, and he was certain she could feel the pounding of his heart under her fingertips. Right now with the adrenaline coursing through his system, all he wanted to do was dip his head down and kiss her. It was the comfort he couldn't give her earlier…and something more. She wasn't just a job anymore, was she? Was he sliding past a line here?

The sound of a dog's bay jolted him out of the moment, and he gave her an apologetic half smile. He reached up and plucked her dangling *kapp* off her head.

"You're going to lose this," he said softly.

She took it from his fingers and looked down at the torn gauze.

"I'm sorry," he added.

"It's okay. Could you keep it in your pocket for me?"

He slipped it into his pocket along with that handkerchief with the smear of her attacker's blood on it. The *kapp* was a personally meaningful piece of her wardrobe, and somehow he felt the honor of being asked to take care of it this way. He felt like he was protecting more than just a piece of cloth. God had somehow entrusted him with something deeper that he couldn't quite identify. It was her hope, her outlook, her belief that she'd get through this.

Dare he think he had been entrusted with her heart, too?

That was too far.

"Okay, so we stay in the trees and then we head that way until we find something that'll help us," he said.

A phone. A friendly stranger. God willing, a police car. It was a mission—a direction. And it was far wiser than kissing her.

He stole a glance at her as they trudged through the trees. She was beautiful in a deep-down kind of way. She was a complicated woman, he realized, and there was something inside of him drawn to the challenge of untangling all of those strings.

Back when he was a kid in his Amish community, back when his parents would whisper late into the night and hide their conversations from him and his siblings, he used to believe that he'd grow up Amish, that he'd marry an Amish girl, and have a houseful of children. And while the girl in his early teenage fantasies hadn't really had much form or substance besides a white apron and *kapp*, he realized that Susanna would fit into those old dreams of Amish life very nicely.

And that was a scary thought. Because he wasn't Amish anymore.

But he hadn't been able to make the Englisher world entirely his own, either. He was a cop—respected, needed— but he was still on the outside of things. That ability to look in from the outside was both his strength as a detective and his source of self-doubt in his personal life. Deep down inside of him, there was still an Amish kid who had hoped with all his heart that he'd have a good Amish life with a community at his back and a wife at his side.

But loyalties had gotten in the way of that.

That was part of what he'd hoped to find at his grandfather's house—some connection to his youth, some answer to that internal, illogical longing. Maybe he'd see some way to put it all to rest so that he could finally fully embrace the life he was actually living.

The rain fell heavier, and they picked up their pace, winding through trees, and eventually coming across what looked like an old bicycle path, which allowed them to walk single file. All the while, Zeke kept an eye on the road, looking for approaching vehicles. But after that ominous blue van, there was nothing.

Ahead, he spotted a familiar little roadside structure. Finally, a break! Amish homes didn't have telephones. Some districts allowed for phones in the barn, and others did not. But the Amish still had need of phones from time to time. They needed to leave each other messages more quickly than the US Postal Service allowed, or to call for a driver to pick them up. They might need to make an appointment with a doctor. Though phones were a necessary tool, the Amish kept that tool outside of the home. In a structure like the one ahead of them.

"There's a phone shanty," Zeke said.

"Thank Gott," she said. "When we call the police, they'll help us?"

"*Yah*," he replied. "I think it's over."

And not a moment too soon. Not only did Zeke need to get Susanna to safety, but he needed to get his own emotions untangled, too. This time with her had been unorthodox. Normally, when he worked with a victim of a crime or an attempted crime, he was emotionally distanced from it all. There was the victim services department to get the support people needed. There were victim advocates and victim support agents. There were solutions in place to help people in their most vulnerable times, but it was never his job. This time around, he didn't have any of those other professionals to rely upon, and he was getting emotionally entangled.

His instructors had warned law enforcement about this. It was important to keep that brusque, professional reserve at all times. Know where your job started and stopped, and allow other professionals to step in and take over. State troopers and detectives saw so much on the job that protecting their emotional equilibrium was of utmost importance—it meant they could get out of bed and go to work tomorrow, too.

So the sooner he could hand Susanna off to a kind, sensitive victim's services coordinator, the better. And he knew that precisely because he didn't want to hand her off. He wanted to stay involved. He wanted to see her safely back into her own world again.

Not my job, he reminded himself.

Except she wasn't feeling like a job anymore. That was the problem.

The rain was driving down in a torrent, and the trees provided only a small amount of shelter. When they got to the little white-sided shanty sitting next to a small gravel area with a hitching post, both Zeke and Susanna were drenched. He pulled open the door, looked inside to find it unoccupied and ushered Susanna into the shelter first. He followed her, tugging the door shut behind them.

Rain drummed on the roof and against a small window that let in some light. It smelled like orange peels inside—someone had eaten an orange in here recently. There was a small table with a phone, some scrap paper, a few stubs of pencils, and a corkboard on the wall behind that held a few messages.

Susanna picked up the phone first, and then she frowned. She tapped on the depressor a couple of times and then handed the receiver to Zeke.

"I think it's dead," she said.

He put it to his ear. Nothing.

"Excuse me," he murmured, slipping past her. Was it unplugged? Was there a loose connection? There had to be a way to fix this! To have come this far and not find a working phone...

He looked down the phone cord, pushed the connector into the wall a little more firmly, and into the base of the phone. There was still no dial tone.

"Oh…" Susanna said, and she pointed to a sign affixed to the corkboard with a thumbtack. It read, *Phone Out of Order* in Pennsylvania Dutch. There were a few personal notes left on the corkboard—someone announcing the birth of their sixth child, another person saying they had extra eggs to sell. But more useful still, there was a small map tacked up there with a little red star in the center.

"Is this a map showing where we are?" he asked.

Susanna nodded. "*Yah*, we do that. It's easier for talking to drivers to explain our location if you have a map."

Zeke untacked the map and took a closer look. After running through the forest it was hard to tell exactly where they were, but seeing these main roads on the map, he had a much better idea.

"Okay, so we can't use this phone, but I'm seeing a rural gas station right here." He tapped the map. "It shouldn't take too long to walk there, and we can use their phone."

Susanna looked over his shoulder, her arm warming a spot on his with her closeness. She was shivering, and Zeke looked out the window at the rain squall.

"We have a choice," he said. "We can wait here until the rain stops and then start walking. Or we can get moving now."

Susanna looked up at him and for a split second he thought she'd choose to wait, but then she frowned.

"In a downpour, we'll be harder to see if anyone is looking for us," she said.

"That's very true." He caught her gaze, and a smile touched her lips.

"I can get warm later," she said. "I think surviving is a higher priority, don't you?"

There was a tough streak in Susanna that impressed him. She could see the priorities, and she wasn't given to panic. Not a lot of civilians had that ability in terrifying times. But she was special—he was realizing that more and more.

"Let's get moving, then," he said.

She was right. It was better to take advantage of the rainstorm than to hide from it.

SEVEN

The rain was cold and soaking, but Susanna would rather walk through rain than wait for that van to come back. Gott had already brought them through so much, and as she walked, following Zeke along the side of the road, she glanced over her shoulder every minute or two, looking for vehicles.

I will lift up mine eyes unto the hills, from whence cometh my help. My help cometh from the Lord, which made heaven and earth...

The familiar psalm she'd memorized as a child started to run through her mind. When she was little, she used to have nightmares. She'd wake up in the night trembling with fear, and she'd clasp her hands together, squeeze her eyes tightly shut and whisper this psalm to herself.

He will not suffer thy foot to be moved: he that keepeth thee will not slumber. Behold, he that keepeth Israel shall neither slumber nor sleep.

She used to do something very daring—something the bishop would never approve. She'd replace the name "Israel" with her own name. *He that keepeth Susanna shall neither slumber nor sleep...*

And while she knew that Gott's word must never be changed, she did believe that Gott was keeping her with the same attention and love as he had for Israel. In her mind, she'd seen Gott's loving care over His people of Israel, and extending over a small Amish girl, too, while she lay in her bed, her sheet over her head and moonlight trickling in through the crack in her curtains.

Back then, her fear was about bad dreams, but now as she walked through that cold drizzle, her fear was much more immediate. Someone was trying to kill her, and that was no imaginary threat. Someone wanted her as dead as Hannah was.

A semitruck came rumbling toward them, headlights gleaming through the rain.

"This guy might help," Zeke said, and he waved his arms over his head to get the driver's attention.

The truck came barreling down the narrow highway toward them, and it didn't slow. Zeke stepped a foot into the road, waving over his head, and the truck swerved around them, sending up a spray of water as it thundered past.

Susanna winced as the dirty water hit her face, and she wiped it off.

"You okay?" Zeke asked, and he used his thumb to take something off her cheek. The gesture was a tender one, and she had to stop herself from leaning into his touch. He was so strong and handsome that it felt too natural to want more of that gentleness from him.

"*Yah*, I'm okay," she said.

She could feel the water seeping through her hair and onto her scalp. Her *kapp* was in his pocket. She'd always been taught that she could not pray without her head covered, but looking out in the downpour, she couldn't help but wonder if Gott would make an exception for her today. She was not praying as a good Amish woman—she was praying as a desperate woman.

"Let's keep walking," he said. "The rain is miserable, but hopefully they won't expect to find us walking down a highway in this downpour."

"*Yah*, let's keep going," she agreed.

Zeke held out his hand, and she hesitated only for a moment. In any other situation, this would be highly inappropriate behavior between herself and any man. But somehow it didn't feel so terrible when taking his hand meant relying on some of that strength to get them to safety.

This was an exception, she told herself. A very extreme exception.

Zeke nudged her onto the inside, leaving him on the side closest to oncoming traffic. Somehow he hadn't slowed down at all through this long, exhausting day. How was he still going at full strength? Her legs were starting to feel shaky, and her stomach rumbled loudly enough that she could hear it.

"*Yah*, me, too," Zeke said in response.

Susanna laughed softly. "Sorry."

"Maybe we can get something to eat at the gas station, too. Something is better than nothing."

"I hope so," she said. "I don't have money, though."

Zeke gave her a wry little smile. "It's on me."

"Okay..." She suddenly felt bashful. "*Danke.*"

As if a little pack of chips or a chocolate bar were worth more than all of the protection he'd given her so far. But it felt a little different now—it felt more personal. Keeping her alive—that was his job. But getting her some food while they waited for some troopers to show up? That felt more like friendship—the kind forged in this terrible emergency.

She was getting emotional, that was all. It was all part of his job, she was sure. No matter how it felt. And very soon this would be over.

The gas station was an old one—a covered area for the pumps, and a small brick shop attached. There were some propane tanks off to one side, and two diesel pumps set farther away—for the trucks? Susanna wasn't sure.

A pickup truck was parked at one pump, a hose leading to the vehicle, but no one standing there to supervise it. Another older farm pickup truck was parked in front of the shop, its wheel wells rusty and its tires muddy. She could feel Zeke's grip on her hand tense. He looked behind them, then released her hand and took a quick turn.

"What's wrong?" she asked.

"I don't know..." He sounded thoughtful. "Nothing, I guess. I'm getting paranoid."

"Do you think they're part of that group?" she asked, her stomach tightening.

"There's no reason to believe they are. Lebanon County is a big place. Not every truck is going to be part of a criminal gang, but they do have patrols out, they said."

And they'd just stumbled across a farm that was crawling with them, and those weren't exactly expected odds, either. Still, they were so close to a phone and rescue. They had to keep going.

They picked up their pace and passed underneath the covered section, winding their way through the gas pumps. The break from the driving rain was a relief. Zeke opened the door to the shop and Susanna stepped in first, but as she did, all eyes turned to them.

There weren't many people in the shop—two Englisher men, one in khaki work pants with reflective stripes, holding a bag of chips and some beef jerky, and the other in blue jeans, paying at the cash register. She spotted the washroom sign at the back of the store, and was reminded quite strongly that she needed the facilities.

The only person who hadn't fallen silent was the young man working behind the till. He wore a red polo shirt, and had the telephone tucked between his cheek and his shoulder, carrying on a conversation with what sounded like his girlfriend.

"Baby, that's not what happened," he was saying, then he said, "Forty-two seventy, please. Credit?"

The man who was supposed to be paying ignored the prompt to pay, his gaze locked on Susanna and Zeke in a way that made her skin crawl.

"Sir?" the worker repeated.

"Credit." The man turned away to pay, breaking that eerily direct look.

"Look, baby, it's not even like that. I met him at Mike's place, and he asked me to help him move. So it's not like that…" the worker was saying. "And when he said he knew you, I had no idea how… Baby… Babe… Are you even listening to me?"

He gave the man his receipt and turned his back, carrying on his argument.

"Is it safe?" she whispered to Zeke. "I'd like to use the washroom, if I could."

"Go ahead," Zeke murmured, and she noticed how his gaze sliced around the store. If those men thought to intimidate with their icy glares, they had nothing on Zeke.

But who would want to intimidate? And why? This was a gas station, not someone's personal property. Was it that she was Amish and Zeke was English? Or was it that they'd been given a description of them, and they matched it? A shiver, along with a trickle of sweat, slipped down her spine.

Susanna headed toward the bathroom and found the door locked. She looked back to see the cashier holding up a key dangling on the end of a piece of wood. She hurried across the store, past both glaring men, and accepted the key with a quick nod. Then she headed back again, trying to ignore those stares.

It didn't have to mean anything. They might just be grumpy and curious. Plenty of people stared at the Amish, and she knew that she was filthy right now and probably was quite a sight. But still…

Gott, even without my prayer kapp, *please hear me.*

Susanna used the key to get into the bathroom and shut the door behind her with a solid thump. She'd planned on washing some of the dirt out of her dress and maybe cleaning herself up in the sink, but she didn't feel comfortable with that now. She used the facilities, washed her hands. Then she used a paper towel to swipe at her face and the more obvious mud on her dress. She looked at her reflection in the mirror. She looked ragged—her hair was dripping wet and some tendrils streaked down the sides of her face. Her bun was coming loose, and she stopped to rewind it into a fresh knot at the back of her head.

Without a *kapp*.

It felt indecent. But still she prayed.

Gott, we need help. Please show us the way!

Some might say that her prayer would bounce off the ceiling, but then a verse came into her mind. *For man looketh on the outward appearance, but the Lord looketh on the heart.* And in her heart, she loved Gott and she longed to live right… She longed to *live.* All she wanted to do was get home again and find some safe corner and never leave it. Somehow—and she couldn't exactly explain how or why—she felt that Gott had heard her. He hadn't brought her this far to drop her now.

Susanna opened the bathroom door and startled to find Zeke's broad back covering her exit. He turned when she opened the door.

"Done?" he asked brusquely.

"Yah."

"Let's go." He had a paper bag, and he put a hand on the small of her back as he propelled her through the store.

The worker was still on the phone, protesting his innocence about something to the woman on the other end of the line, and the two men were still there, too. They hadn't left yet. Their steely gazes followed them just the same as earlier, except one of the men frowned, then pulled out a cell phone and put it up to his ear, his gaze still locked on her.

"Aren't we using the phone?" she whispered as Zeke opened the door for her. She exited first, and she got the distinct feeling that he was walking behind her as a sort of shield between her and those men.

That telephone was their link to police backup. It was their only chance at safety, but Zeke hadn't slowed, and she could feel the urgency in his touch on her back.

"No," he said. "I'm not waiting around there to ask, either. I've got some snacks. Let's keep moving."

"But the police—"

When she looked over her shoulder, that man on the cell phone was talking, his hard eyes still locked on her. He was reporting something, and she had a strong feeling it wasn't to the police.

Zeke hated every step he had to take away from that telephone, but his hackles were still up from his encounter with those men. They'd reported them—there was no doubt about that.

"Are we in danger?" Susanna asked.

"Just keep walking."

Because he wasn't sure. They were on foot, and if those men were connected to whoever was after Susanna, they didn't have much time to get themselves out of sight and somewhere safe.

But where?

"Here, I bought some chocolate bars and some bottles of juice. We need energy." He opened the bag and she pulled out a chocolate bar.

"*Danke*," she said, opening the wrapper and taking a bite. He did the same. He was hungry, but they needed some quick energy if they were going to keep moving. Adrenaline would only take them so far. They'd need some proper food soon—from a restaurant in Felder, maybe? He had to think ahead, form a plan. But he was starting to feel bleary.

Gott, we need Your help, he prayed. *Please, show me the next step.*

He was one man—a determined man who was willing to put himself bodily between her and danger, but still… only one. Was he going to be enough to keep her out of the hands of the men who wanted her dead or alive?

He had to be!

"Okay, so I need to fill you in on what I heard at the farm," Zeke said. There was a gravel road that led off the main drag, and with a bend in the road hiding them from view, he tugged her in that direction. The rain had slowed down to a light mist. "The leader of this group seems to be named Daniel Schaber. They talk about him like he's calling the shots—at least locally. I don't know who he is, but at least it's a name to follow once I have the police resources at my fingertips again."

"I've never heard of him."

"Me, neither. Not by name, at least." He looked over his shoulder again—all was quiet. For now. "But he is definitely part of the group here. They were talking like he was inside the farmhouse, and he'd checked the burned-out car and discovered we weren't in it. So I'm thinking he's one of the men chasing us. I had a hunch he was the one in control—the boss."

Hunches didn't stand up in court, but they did keep people alive. Susanna had an analytical mind, and it was useful to bounce this information off of her. Unorthodox, definitely, but useful. They walked a little farther in silence, shoes crunching over gravel. The rain was still coming down in a steady, driving drizzle, but he did his best to ignore the cold and discomfort.

"Why are you telling me all this?" she asked. "You'll be the one reporting it."

"If we get separated, I want you to tell the first trooper you see," he said.

"I don't like the sound of that."

"Whether I tell them, or you tell them, the police need to know."

And if he had to make good on his private vow to stand between her and danger, and he didn't survive it, the police needed that information.

They walked in silence for a couple more minutes, before Susanna broke it.

"Zeke, are your parents glad they left?" she asked.

"Are they glad?" he asked, trying to change gears. "Uh—my *daet* passed away last year. He was very certain that he'd done the right thing for us."

And they'd still called him Daet, not the anglicized *Dad.* That would never change.

"Why?" she asked.

"He didn't believe in everything Amish," he replied. "He disagreed on some theological points."

"Like?"

He laughed softly. "I don't want to offend you with my *daet*'s way of seeing things."

"It won't offend me," she said. "I'm curious."

"Well..." He looked over his shoulder once more. No one was following yet. He sighed, and thought back to the long discussions his parents used to have, their Bibles open as they flipped from passage to passage. "They didn't believe that we had to stay away from technological advancements, and they disagreed with shunning for anything but the most extreme cases. They believed in education for me and my siblings."

She was silent.

"Susanna, I'm not trying to change your mind on any of your beliefs," he said.

"And your *mamm*?" she asked. "Does she think they did the right thing by leaving?"

"It was a long time ago," he replied. "She loved my *daet* something fierce, and she believed her place was by his side. She backs up his memory. They made that move together. But there are some things she misses about Amish life."

"Like what?" Susanna asked.

"The same things I miss, I suppose," he said. "The strong sense of community—actually being able to rely on your neighbor. And there's the focus on God above all else. The Amish are right that all the conveniences and rushing around does distract you from what matters most."

"You mean you couldn't go to a neighbor if you needed help with something?" Susanna asked.

"Not really." He glanced over his shoulder again at the empty road behind him. They were curving to the left, and the main road was now out of sight, which meant they were out of sight, too. What he wouldn't do for a helpful neighbor right about now. "In English culture, everyone takes care of themselves and their own families. You are a respectable citizen if you keep your problems to yourself and don't bother others with them."

"That sounds awfully lonesome," she said.

"Yah." It had been, especially when he hadn't been raised to that way of thinking. People said that the Amish were isolated from the rest of America, but he'd never felt more isolated than when they'd left the Amish fold.

"Do you ever think about coming back?" she asked.

"I'm a state trooper, Susanna. There are no Amish law enforcement officers."

"I know. It would mean…quitting, I suppose. That's too much to ask, isn't it?"

"My job is all I have," he said, and he immediately regretted the honest answer. He was supposed to be reassuring, not laying his own insecurities bare. "I shouldn't say that—"

"You should, if it's true," she countered.

He cast her a smile, but then, just ahead, he spotted a horse coming around the bend. It was pulling a buggy, and the timing was so serendipitous that his heart skipped a beat.

"Speaking of neighbors," he murmured.

"Maybe he'll help us," Susanna said.

"Let's hope."

Zeke had grown a little jaded over the last twenty years. People had their own concerns. The sight of two people in need didn't necessarily nudge them toward helping. They were cautious, and for good reason these days. Good Samaritans could get badly hurt or taken advantage of. Police warned people not to stop and help someone who looked desperate or stranded—it could be a ruse. But this time around, he was the desperate one in need of help.

The man in the buggy had a brown beard, not too long. He leaned forward to get a better look at them, and when Susanna waved at him, he reined in.

"Are you folks okay?" he called in English.

"*Nee*, we aren't!" Susanna said in Pennsylvania Dutch. "We need help very badly. It's a long story, but if you would give us a ride, we would be so grateful."

"Where are you going?" he asked her in the same language she'd used. "And who is this Englisher?"

"He's a friend," she said. "And he's no danger to me. But I am in a lot of trouble. We need to get to a phone."

"You look like you need a mite more than that," he replied. "It's raining. Get in the back, and you can tell me while I drive."

She turned to Zeke and started to translate their conversation. "He said—"

"*Yah*, I understood," he replied in Pennsylvania Dutch.

A smile touched her lips. She'd momentarily forgotten that it was his mother tongue, too. They didn't waste time getting into the back of the buggy, and the back was preferable as it kept them out of sight. The man flicked the reins and they started forward again with a familiar jerk, just as a pickup truck came toward them the way they'd come. Zeke put a hand out to push Susanna out of sight through the small open square in the back. He couldn't see the driver, but he wasn't taking chances, either.

"My name is Aaron Petersheim," the Amish man said.

"I'm Susanna, and this is Zeke," Susanna said. "*Danke* so much for giving us a lift. We're so tired and hungry."

"Where do you need to go?" he asked.

"Into town," Zeke said.

"I'm not headed there," Aaron replied. "It's a half hour buggy ride the other direction. Besides, a tree went down over the road that leads into town, and until it's chopped up and removed, there will be no getting past. But you said you're hungry?"

"And dirty and tired and…" Susanna's voice trembled. "*Yah*, we need help."

Zeke wasn't sure how bedraggled they looked to others. Susanna's dress was mud-streaked, and without her *kapp*, she looked like she'd been through the wringer. He couldn't look much better. But if a tree was blocking the road into town, he had to wonder how providential that was.

"So, then?" the man asked, glancing back. "What's the trouble?"

"It's probably better that we don't give you the whole story," Zeke said. "But I am a state trooper, and some very nasty people are after this young woman. I'm trying to get her to safety."

"Oh my."

"We could use somewhere to be out of sight for a few hours," Susanna said. "And maybe a meal, if you have enough to share?"

"We have plenty to share," he replied. "And my wife at home can help you get sorted out, I'm sure. You both look quite a mess."

"We know it," Zeke said. "*Danke*. We do appreciate the help."

He looked out the back square window of the buggy again and he pulled the rain flap down to cover it. Another vehicle rumbled past them, coming from the other direction.

"Those Englishers are looking for something…or someone," Aaron said soberly. "They're looking all over the side of the road. That one stopped. They're interested in something on the ground."

Zeke swallowed. They were looking for Zeke and Susanna, trying to find some clue as to where they'd disappeared. Would Aaron look suspicious to them? Would they think to look into the back of a buggy?

"Ah, that's what," Aaron said. "They found a *kapp*. Yours?"

Zeke checked his pocket—Susanna's *kapp* was gone. He winced. He'd promised her that he'd care for it, and he felt like he'd let her down. The handkerchief was still there, though.

"*Yah*, hers," he said, and he met Susanna's solemn gaze with apology.

"It's okay," she said softly. "It will give them something to focus on. Maybe they'll go check the woods again."

"Then I won't be asking questions," Aaron said, "and I can't very well put you off on the side of the road in any good conscience."

"What will you do?" Zeke asked.

"I will pray," he replied, and then he quoted a verse that Zeke knew well. "*I will put thee in a clift of the rock, and will cover thee with my hand.* May Gott cover us."

"Do you have a phone shanty we can use?" Zeke asked.

"*Nee*, ours has been out of order for some time."

"A neighboring one?" Susanna asked hopefully.

"We had a rash of vandalism this spring," he replied. "Some local youths thought it was terribly funny to cut telephone cables and paint graffiti on the shanties. We've painted them all clean again, but the telephone wires…we haven't fixed those yet. I'm sorry. I can offer a hot meal, though. And I'm sure my wife would share a *kapp* with you."

Color touched Susanna's cheeks. She must be feeling the lack of her head covering. To the Englishers it was nothing but fashion. For an Amish woman, it was a sign of propriety.

"*Danke*, that would be very kind," she said. "You're a good neighbor."

A neighbor, right when one was needed most. If this man was an answer to Susanna's prayer, then it had been a swift answer, indeed.

Another truck came past them much more slowly, and Zeke and Susanna bent down in the back. Aaron nodded a greeting to whomever was peering in at him.

They were circling like hawks, spiraling in closer and closer to their prey. Zeke could only pray that this good Amish man's neighborliness didn't end up getting him killed.

When the truck sped up and passed them, Zeke exhaled a pent-up breath.

"Best stay low back there," Aaron said quietly. "That man looked like evil incarnate."

EIGHT

Susanna had never been to this church district before. But she did know that they were Swartzentruber Amish— the most conservative of the Amish sects—and when they pulled into his drive she could see the difference already. The house was smaller, and there was an outhouse stationed between the house proper and the stable. In her home community, they had indoor plumbing and their houses were a bit larger and more sturdily constructed.

There was a barn farther off, the smell of which confirmed it as a chicken farm. The Petersheims must sell eggs and butcher chickens. Susanna's grandparents had been chicken farmers, so she recognized the setup. The front yard had freshly mown grass, wet from the rain. There were two gardens, both dedicated to vegetables, not flowers, but they were nicely weeded and the visible earth was black. There was a warm, comfortable feel to the little farm. This was a home that was lovingly tended.

The rain had finally stopped, and some rays of sunlight sparkled through the clouds. The side door burst open and two little girls came hopping down the rain-wet stairs, *kapp* strings fluttering out behind them.

"Daet is home! Daet is home!" they sang, and Susanna

couldn't help but smile. A long time ago, she'd done the same thing when her *daet* came home from some outing.

But then her stomach dropped. This was a home with small children—a tender little family—and she and Zeke were on the run from some very dangerous men.

Susanna looked over to find Zeke's expression similarly sober. They climbed down from the back of the buggy, Susanna's wet dress clinging uncomfortably to her legs and arms. The girls skidded to a stop, eyes wide.

"These are some friends, girls," Aaron said. "Go call Mamm."

The girls went running back into the house, their piping voices heard outside as they shouted for their mother to come outside and see the strangers.

"It's all right," Aaron said. "Come inside."

"We won't be staying long," Zeke said. "We'll be on our way again soon."

"No need to rush," Aaron replied. "You need rest."

Zeke didn't answer, but she thought she understood his worry. This family could not be harmed because Aaron had given them aid in their time of need. The Amish prided themselves on being good neighbors, but sometimes a person's need went beyond that cup of sugar, and there was a deeper cost to helping.

"Hello, hello!" A young woman came outside and held the door open.

"Maria, this is Zeke and Susanna. I found them on the road. They are…" Aaron looked over at them with mild worry in his eyes. "They are in trouble."

"With the law?" Maria whispered.

"*Nee*," Zeke said quickly. "I'm a Pennsylvania State Police trooper, and I'm trying to get this woman to safety. It's complicated, but this is my badge."

He pulled it out and Maria looked it over, but she likely had the same problem that Susanna did—she wouldn't know a fake from the authentic. Maria cast her husband an uncomfortable look.

"They need our help, Maria," Aaron said quietly. "I could not send this woman out onto the road again. It would be wrong."

The implication was that he'd have sent Zeke away much more easily, and Susanna's heart went out to Zeke. He was just as stranded as she was. He was just as desperate, and in just as much danger. The men following them would kill Zeke as easily as they'd kill her.

Maria's lips thinned, and she and her husband exchanged a long, meaningful look. A decision was being made there— one of those unspoken conversations between a married couple. Then Maria sighed.

"Please, come inside." She stepped back. "Girls, go upstairs."

The girls disappeared, and Susanna tried to let Zeke go first into the house as would be proper by Amish manners, but Zeke put a hand on her back and ushered her in ahead of him. Maria's eyes widened at the intimate touch. Susanna would have some explaining to do evidently.

"I lost my *kapp*," Susanna said softly, suddenly feeling bashful with her uncovered head and a man who was not her husband touching her waist. She felt like she was setting a terrible example for those little girls.

"Come upstairs. I'll get you into a fresh dress and *kapp*," Maria said. "You look like you've been through something."

"Danke." Susanna had to blink back a mist of grateful tears. It was generous of this woman to look at it that way.

Maria led the way up the stairs, and Susanna followed, leaving the low rumble of men's voices below. She could make out Zeke's voice as he answered some questions, and she realized that his bass voice was strangely comforting to her. And now familiar, too. With Zeke, she knew she'd be safe. For whatever reason, he seemed to be staking his very life upon her safety, and while she didn't understand why, she was deeply grateful for it. The police might not be welcome in their communities, but Zeke seemed to be different, and it wasn't just his Amish upbringing. Most people would say he knew enough to know better. She looked over her shoulder just before she got to the top of the stairs, and Zeke looked over at the same time. Their gazes met, and while she couldn't explain why, she felt in her bones that he would see her through this.

The top floor of the little house had two large bedrooms, and the little girls were huddled in one of them, watching Maria and Susanna wide-eyed. They held hands, their bare, dirty feet dangling off the end of one bed.

"Come into Mamm and Daet's room with us," Maria said, holding out a hand to her daughters.

The girls came pattering into the other bedroom and Maria shut the door. The children's dresses were mussed with dirt from playing, and the bottoms of their feet were brown from running outdoors without their shoes on.

"Let's see," Maria said as she looked at Susanna. "You're taller than me, but I have one dress that I think will suit you. My sister forgot it on her last visit." She pulled a dark green dress out of her closet and held it up for Susanna's inspection.

"*Danke*," Susanna said. "I do appreciate this."

"Let me help you," Maria said, and she bent down to start pulling straight pins out of Susanna's dress and the few safety pins that she'd used at the waist and bust.

"Get the pins, Esther," Maria said, and the taller girl fetched a cut glass bowl filled with pins.

"Get me the washing basin."

There was a basin and water jug on a bedside table, and the older girl poured some water into it while the littler girl fetched a cloth. Maria used a thick white bar of soap and rubbed some onto the dampened cloth. The water was cold, but it did feel good to get the dirt off her skin and to freshen herself up a little bit.

"Is he really police?" Maria asked softly.

"*Yah*, he is. He saved my life."

"What happened?"

"Someone tried to—" She looked down at the little girls. "I don't want to scare them. But someone tried to get me to take a ride in a van." She tried to lighten her tone. "And that is a very dangerous thing to do, girls. Never, ever get into a stranger's vehicle."

Maria's face whitened. She understood.

"My cousin's daughter was…in a similar situation," she said. "She got away, though."

"Is her name Rachel?"

Maria nodded.

"I heard what happened," Susanna said.

This was how adults discussed frightening things in front of children. They skipped around it, hinted and gave just enough information for the adults to glean their meaning.

"The same thing—" Maria swallowed. "Is that what happened to you, too?"

"*Yah*. But Zeke intercepted them and saved me. They are who's after me. We don't entirely know why they want me, but… Zeke is helping me."

"Thanks to Gott for His mercies," Maria murmured. "Where will you go from here?"

"We need a telephone. Do you know where we can find one?"

She shook her head. "The closest Amish telephone right now is in Felder. We have to drive all the way to town to use it. Ours were vandalized. There is one at the gas station, but they don't like us to use it. They say it's for business use only."

Not really if that employee was arguing with his girlfriend on the phone there, but she understood that some businesses weren't sympathetic to the Amish's unique needs.

"I was hoping there might be one closer…someone with a phone in their barn?"

"Not in our district," Maria replied. "Our bishop is very strict about that. You won't find one in an Amish farm, at least. You'd have to try an English farm."

They had—and that had been incredibly dangerous. There was also another girl on that English farm, and Susanna swallowed hard.

"Whatever you do, keep your little girls close," she whispered. "Don't let them go anywhere without you. But be careful for yourself, too."

Maria nodded. "I'd hoped that this danger had stopped."

"I'm sorry to tell you this, but it seems that it's getting worse," Susanna whispered. "Much worse. And we need to contact the police so that they can step in."

"The police… I don't know about your community, but we don't do with police here. Gott gives us the wisdom to handle things on our own. We don't need government intervention."

"This is bigger than we can handle, Maria," Susanna whispered. "My cousin was Hannah Stutzman." The name took a moment to register in Maria's eyes, but then it did, and her face fell. "And I don't know why, but the same men are after me. They have not only numbers on their sides, but weapons, vehicles…even a helicopter. They are bigger than we can handle alone. We need Englisher help."

Maria nodded, her face white. "A helicopter?"

"*Yah*. But you've heard about the girls going missing. You must—" She looked over at the little girls again; they just stared at her.

"Girls, have you swept your room yet?" Maria raised her eyebrows.

"*Nee…*"

"Best go get it done, then."

The girls slipped away, and their mother deflated a little bit as she turned back to Susanna. "*Yah*, we've heard plenty."

"Do you know anything about these men?" Susanna asked.

"Two girls in our community were walking together and a blue van came up beside them," Maria said. "The girls knew the man driving it—he'd been around our community a little bit, offering driver services. He'd been driving their grandmother to some appointments in town."

A blue van—she knew that van rather well now, herself.

"They knew him?" Susanna gasped.

"*Yah*. And then he offered them a ride, but they said no thank you. Then he pressed, saying they should trust him and stop being rude. One of them started to get in, but she saw another man inside the van, and she pulled back. The men tried to grab the girls, but they managed to get away and they ran all the way home."

"Did their parents report it?"

"To the bishop? *Yah* To the police? *Nee*. That is our business."

So there were other abduction attempts. Not just her and the girls they knew about. There were more, and those girls Maria told her about had known the man who'd tried to abduct them. As for herself, she'd never seen her attacker before in her life. And they now had a name for a leader of this group, and he also seemed to drive a blue van. It couldn't be a coincidence. Didn't Zeke say that there was normally a connection?

"Did he have a name?" Susanna asked.

The other woman just shook her head.

"Did they call him Daniel, perhaps?" she pressed. "Or Danny?"

The woman shook her head again. "No one said."

Maria went to her dresser and picked up a *kapp* from where it sat on a doily—a place of honor. It wasn't the style that Susanna's community used—the gauzy, heart-shaped covering. This was the Swartzentruber *kapp*, made of denser material that kept its shape.

"Oh, Maria, it's your good church *kapp*, isn't it?"

"It's the only other *kapp* I own," Maria said. "And I will not send you away with nothing to cover your head while I have two."

"This is very Christian of you," Susanna said.

"Gott wouldn't hear my prayers if I refused it," Maria said simply. "He sent you to us, and we will help."

It was simple here—if there was good to do, a person must do it.

There was a little tap on the bedroom door, and Maria opened it. Her daughters stood in the hallway.

"Our bedroom is clean," the older one said.

"Good. That was quick. Well done." She cast her daughters a reassuring smile.

Susanna unwound her hair, and one of the little girls picked up a comb from the dresser.

"We'll help," they said.

"*Danke*," Susanna said, and she sat on the edge of the bed. The girl clambered up behind her and the older girl began to comb out her long hair with smooth, satisfying strokes. They probably did this for their *mamm* and had learned to comb out long hair very well.

Still, she couldn't help but keep thinking about those girls knowing the man in the blue van. He'd been a driver… It was more information than they'd had before.

Aaron stood at the counter slicing a fluffy loaf of whole grain bread. Fluffy and whole grain didn't usually go together, but they did for this loaf. Aaron's wife must be one good baker. On the black woodstove, a pot of soup was simmering. It smelled like beef barley to Zeke. His *mamm* made a similar soup that he'd always liked. Aaron pulled some sandwich meat out of their icebox. In Zeke's childhood, they'd had a similar setup, but he knew that the more moderate Old Order Amish used gas-powered refrigerators now. The Swartzentruber Amish stuck to the old ways, though. All of them.

Efficient in the kitchen, Aaron made a quick plate of ham and cheese sandwiches, and deposited them in the center of the table, then added some stoneware bowls. As he worked, Zeke went over to the window to look outside.

"Is there any way to get to Felder besides the main road?" Zeke asked.

"There are some back roads you can take that will get you to town," Aaron replied, but a worried look creased his brow. "It takes longer, of course. Or you could go cross-field— that's another option."

Zeke perked up at that. "Cross-field?"

"*Yah*. You head west across our cow pasture, and then pass into my neighbor's oat field. You'll see a stand of trees that separates that oat field from another pasture. You pass through the trees, cross that pasture in the northerly direction. You'll cross another section of trees—and when you come out on the other side, you'll see Felder from there."

Zeke looked over toward the cow pasture. If they took roads, there was the constant worry that they'd be spotted by the wrong vehicle, or if Aaron gave them a ride, there was a risk to Aaron's safety, too, but cross-field was an excellent solution. It would be faster than walking by road, and would keep them out of sight for the most part.

"I think we'll try to go cross-field," Zeke said. "No need to put you folks out more than we already have. I appreciate what you are doing for us, Aaron. Once we eat, we'll be on our way again."

Aaron's shoulders lowered a little bit, and his expression softened. He was relieved, Zeke could tell. And he didn't blame him one bit.

"Do you want dry clothes?" Aaron asked. "You might… blend in better."

"If you have something to spare," Zeke replied.

"*Yah*. I'll get you some pants, suspenders and a shirt. Also a hat—I've got an old one. If anyone sees you from a distance, they'll think you're Amish."

Zeke smiled ruefully. *Yah*, he could look and sound Amish enough. The only thing he was missing was the haircut, but maybe that was a detail these thugs wouldn't notice.

The women came back downstairs then. Susanna was dressed in a dark green dress—a bit different in cut from the blue dress she was wearing before. She'd blend into fields and trees a whole lot better wearing green, but it was pretty on her, too. There was something about those modest Amish dresses that was firmly engrained in his psyche. They represented home and safety and his boyish hopes for his future.

"Okay?" Susanna asked, spreading her arms.

"*Yah*, you look very *schee*." Pretty. It was utterly true, but he noticed the uncomfortable way Maria looked away, and he knew he'd crossed propriety lines there.

"Let's get you into something dry, yourself," Aaron said. "Then we'll eat."

Upstairs in the bedroom, it didn't take long for Zeke to peel off his wet, dirty clothes and get into a dry pair of broadfall pants complete with suspenders, and a white long-sleeved shirt. The shirt was a little small, but it would do if he rolled the sleeves up his forearms. Strange how comfortable it was to get back into Amish garb again. He hadn't worn it since they'd left when he was a teenager.

Zeke glanced around the bedroom. The open closet revealed only two dresses, and when Aaron opened a dresser drawer, there was only one pair of pants inside. Zeke seemed to be wearing his only other pair. Aaron and Maria were not giving out of their plenty. They were giving their widow's mite, so to speak.

"*Danke* again, Aaron," Zeke said. "I have a few dollars in my wallet here—"

"It wouldn't be a kindness if I expected repayment," Aaron replied. "Accept it in the spirit it was given."

Zeke nodded his thanks, not quite trusting himself to words. He prayed Gott would bless this couple many times over for their generosity.

"And a hat." Aaron passed him a slightly worn straw hat.

"Now, let's eat," Aaron said.

Zeke didn't need more invitation than that. This would be their first proper meal in two days.

Zeke took a seat at the table next to Susanna, and he caught the amused little smile when she noted his clothing change.

"You'd almost pass as Amish," she murmured.

"Almost." But not quite.

They bowed their heads for a silent grace and when Aaron cleared his throat, they all raised their heads and dished up. Zeke and Susanna ate ravenously, and Maria filled both of their bowls with soup twice more. The little girls watched them wide-eyed, but Zeke was too hungry to hold back.

"What's that?" one of the little girls asked, hopping down from her seat.

A moment later, Zeke heard what she'd heard—an engine in the drive.

"No!" Zeke barked, and the girl froze. "I'm sorry—" He stood up and went cautiously to the window. He pulled down the green blind and then peeked around the side of it. A blue van.

"Susanna," he said, his voice low. "We need to leave *now*."

Susanna stood up, her cheeks blanching.

"Thank you for everything," she whispered.

"Get your girls upstairs," Zeke ordered, "and we'll leave. Do you have a back way out?"

Aaron pointed out a back door that led into the garden, and Zeke and Susanna slammed their feet into their shoes and ran. He pulled the door quietly shut behind them, and scanned the backyard.

"We need to get to that field," he whispered, noting that there was one large round bale of hay not far from the fence.

But between the house and the big bale was the outhouse and the stable. They could use those for cover until they got to the bale and open field.

The blue van had parked next to the house and the man who'd tried to abduct Susanna got out and went to the door. Aaron opened it immediately and stepped outside. The courage this Amish man possessed was impressive.

"Can I help you?" Aaron asked in Pennsylvania Dutch.

"We're looking for..." The man paused. "We need to look for... We—" His Pennsylvania Dutch was limited, but the man could speak it. That was a detail to note.

"*Yah?*" Aaron pressed, not switching to English.

"Two people—a man and a woman," the man said in Pennsylvania Dutch. "We think we— Do you speak English?"

"A man and a woman?" Aaron pressed, sticking to Deutsch, and Zeke couldn't help but smile at that man's brilliant distraction.

Zeke took Susanna's arm, and they silently slipped from behind the house over to the outhouse. He pulled Susanna into his arms to keep them from sight, and he peeked around the side to see that both men were fixed on Aaron now.

They dashed again, this time to the stable, and they stopped there.

"I need to see that they're safe," Zeke whispered. "You go on to that bale, and hide behind it. If I don't get out of this, you need to cross the field and the oat field beyond it, find the next tree line heading north, and keep going. You'll hit Felder and can call for help."

"What are you going to do?" she whispered fiercely.

He had a choice now—tell her something reassuring that would make her feel better or...

"I have six bullets," he whispered. He'd opted for the truth. "I'm not letting anything happen to those people."

Susanna froze. This went against all of her Anabaptist beliefs. They were pacifists. They believed in sacrificing themselves before ever taking another human life. But Zeke wasn't about to sacrifice that family. He had the ability to save them, and his conscience wouldn't allow him to leave them defenseless.

"Go!" he whispered. "This is on my conscience, not yours."

And if men died today, he was a state police trooper who would answer for it both to the law and before Gott.

Susanna's gaze flicked from him to the house beyond, and she gave him one unfathomable look before she turned and ran quietly to the fence, slipped through the rails and disappeared behind the bale.

What did she think of him now?

But he didn't have time to worry about that. He focused on the conversation over at the house.

"Did you see a man and a woman?" the man shouted, pulling out a gun and pointing it into Aaron's face.

Zeke flicked the thumb snap and eased his side arm out of the holster. With one hand underneath for stability, he crept forward.

"There is no one in my house but my family!" Aaron roared back. "This is my home! Who are you? What do you want with me?"

Not a single lie uttered, and Aaron didn't back down, either. The man muttered something and reholstered his weapon.

"Then you won't mind if we check," he said, and he motioned for the other man to go inside. Zeke's heart stuttered to a stop. There were two little girls in that house, and if they so much as laid a finger on them—

The man emerged a couple of minutes later.

"Nothing. They're clear."

Without another word, the two men went back to the vehicle and got inside. Zeke pulled back, taking slow, deep breaths to keep his body calm, and when the van backed out of the drive, Zeke looked over to where Aaron stood. The Swartzentruber man was shaking now, and sank down onto his haunches.

Zeke wanted to comfort him, but Zeke's presence wouldn't make things any safer for them now. The door opened and Maria came out, rushing to her husband's side.

"Gott, protect them," Zeke whispered, and he holstered his own weapon, and slipped across the grass toward the fence. He slipped through the rails and joined Susanna in its shadow.

"Okay," he whispered. "Now we get as far from here as possible."

"They have little girls," she breathed.

"And that's why we need to stop these men with all of the power that law enforcement has," he said. "We need backup, Susanna."

She nodded.

"Let's go," he said, and he pushed the straw hat lower on his head, took her shaking hand in his, and they started out across the field.

From a distance, they'd blend in like an Amish couple who belonged.

"Would you have killed them?" Susanna asked, her voice low.

"*Yah*," he replied. God forgive him, he would have.

She didn't say anything else, but she didn't release his hand, either. Yes, he would have killed them if he'd had to, but they hadn't forced the issue. Besides, stopping one or two men wouldn't stop the wave of crime and fear. It wouldn't bring backup, and mostly would bring in more criminal reinforcements. And retaliation against this family.

The town of Felder was now within reach. He had to focus on the next step.

NINE

They walked briskly through the fields, looking back over their shoulders from time to time, but no one followed. The knee-high oats were soft and green, and the breeze rippled over the field like a pool of water. Another day, another time, this would have been peaceful.

Susanna looked back over her shoulder again. The little farmhouse had disappeared from view, and they turned now toward a stretch of trees. She held on to Zeke's hand—mostly because he helped her to walk faster, she told herself. But there was comfort there, too. Zeke stood between her and some very bad people, and while the Amish didn't work in law enforcement, they did accept that Englishers helped them with police protection when absolutely necessary and protection beyond their borders. They weren't naive about that.

Perhaps she was being naive about Zeke, though. This man wasn't Amish anymore. That was the thought that nagged at the back of her mind. The fact that he'd been raised Amish had given them a bridge between their differences, but if he was willing to kill two men, even in the defense of a family, then he didn't hold those Amish values anymore.

The Amish were nonviolent pacifists. They saw the

value in all human life, and believed those men with evil intent were men in need of salvation. Easier to say when they weren't murdering her cousin and chasing her down, though. If they'd succeeded in kidnapping her, would she have been willing to kill one of them to escape their clutches? It was a sobering thought that the ideals she'd held dear for a lifetime could be shaken in the space of two traumatizing days.

"Are you all right?" Zeke asked.

She considered telling him she was fine as they approached the tree line. Zeke looked in all directions, then tugged her after him into the slim patch of forest. She could see the light coming through the trees about ten yards ahead.

"I'm Amish," she said. "I'm supposed to be willing to sacrifice my own life for that of my enemy."

"Don't worry," he said gruffly. "I'm not sacrificing you for anything."

His words were comforting, but he didn't understand. He'd left the Amish life and had lived English ever since. They had different sensibilities, and they didn't stop at the lines where the Amish consciences did. Zeke had been trained in law enforcement, and he lived in a world she doubted she'd ever fully understand, either.

"Don't you remember what we're supposed to stand for?" she asked.

We. She hadn't meant to lump him in with her own people, but he had been raised Amish. He should know, at the very least. Even if he didn't agree. Even if he hadn't made vows to their church and faith.

Zeke looked down at her, and then his granite face softened. "We can do both, Susanna. We can defend the innocent and use compassion when dealing with our enemies."

"You said you'd have killed them."

"If pushed to the absolute limit, I wouldn't have had a choice," he replied. "We do our best to never take a life, if we can help it, you know. We aren't monsters. I'm a pretty good shot, and I'm capable of shooting a leg."

That hadn't occurred to her. Perhaps there was some wiggle room there in which to survive.

"You have a point," she agreed.

"And I do understand how hard this is for you," he said quietly. "I won't make you make those kinds of choices, if I can help it."

She nodded mutely, her emotions stuck like a rock in her throat. In one terrifying moment, with one knee-jerk reaction, could she be toying with her own salvation? She was scared. She wanted to live. But their ancestors had sacrificed their very lives for their enemies. She was supposed to be willing to do the same. And what if, when the moment came, she didn't? She believed that life was a series of lessons, and it was also a testing ground for their faith. Was Gott testing hers?

"Susanna?"

She pulled out of her thoughts and looked up again. His earnest gaze was locked on her.

"I meant it," he said. "I would not have sacrificed you. If I had to choose between my life and yours, I'd choose yours."

She believed him. Tears misted her eyes. That wasn't quite the solution to her moral dilemma that she'd been looking for, but it seemed to solve the issue for him.

"Come on," he said. "Once we get through these trees, we should be able to see Felder. We're almost there."

As they walked into the outskirts of Felder, Zeke's feet were sore, and a blister he'd rubbed yesterday had burst.

But that little town was a sight for sore eyes. It was both their refuge after days of running for their lives, and a flood of childhood memories all combined into one emotionally complex package.

Zeke swallowed against a lump in his throat. He'd had so many experiences here—the foundational kind, like standing in line at the credit union with his *daet*, or picking up an order from the farm supply shop when he was twelve, and feeling like a grown man with responsibilities. There was the pull of memories and the push of his parents' shunning, and he wished he could feel just one thing about this place instead of a knot of conflicting emotions.

Zeke and Susanna had to get onto the main road to walk into town, but in Amish clothing, they blended in better than he could have hoped. No one gave them a second look as they came up to Rosie's Diner at the town limits. Rosie's hadn't changed at all. The sign had faded a good deal, but the rest was the same.

"I remember this place," Zeke said.

"*Yah?* From when you were young?"

"*Yah.* I went there with my family for pie on one of my birthdays. It was a special treat. We didn't get to do that kind of thing too often."

Instead of a new scooter, he'd asked for this treat as a family. He'd wanted to have something special, all of them together. The waitress had found out it was Zeke's fourteenth birthday, and she'd put a candle in his slice of lemon meringue pie, and the cook came out from the back, and the other waitress came from the other side of the diner, and they'd all sung the birthday song to him.

That was the year that their family had left the community.

Zeke looked over his shoulder as a pickup truck passed

them. A stony-faced man looked at them through an open window on his way by. Zeke dropped his gaze and fought back the urge to grab Susanna's hand again. Amish couples didn't go around holding hands.

Just a farmer. Just an Amish farmer. He silently willed the man to believe it.

The pickup truck carried on and didn't slow down. He heard Susanna's soft sigh of relief.

"We'll use the phone at Rosie's," he said. "We're close, Susanna. This is almost over."

He'd get her into protective custody, and send a swarm of police over to that farmhouse. May God protect that Mennonite girl those thugs had snatched until law enforcement could get there.

Zeke picked up his pace. His foot hurt, but he pushed the pain to the back of his mind. He could heal later—they weren't done yet.

When they got to the diner, another vehicle passed them, slowing down considerably this time, and Zeke had a feeling they'd been spotted again, but he wasn't walking away from a phone this time. They were in town, had witnesses, and would not survive another attempt to run. They were losing strength, and they were severely outnumbered.

He pulled open the diner door and Susanna rushed inside ahead of him. A welcome blast of air-conditioning hit him, and all of the exhaustion he'd been carrying with him seemed to descend on him at once. But they weren't free of this yet.

There was the clatter of dishes coming from the back kitchen, and a swinging door suddenly pushed open and a waitress came out with a tray held aloft in one hand. Several plates of hot food were arranged there, and she breezed past, heading toward a table in the middle of the restaurant. It was an Amish family, one that looked familiar on a heart level, like he and his family must have looked on his fourteenth birthday. That all swept through his mind in a blink, though.

It didn't matter how tired he was. Zeke stepped up to the front counter.

"I need a phone," Zeke said to a different waitress who had just stepped up with two menus in her hands. "A phone. Please, it's an emergency. I need a phone now!"

"Um—" She put down the menus and handed over a cordless landline telephone.

Zeke looked out the window at the SUV that had pulled into the parking lot. His gut told him that vehicle was trouble. He pushed back the rising anxiety and dialed 911.

"Nine-one-one. What is your emergency?"

"I need police at Rosie's Diner in Felder, *stat*! I am Trooper Zeke Esch from Troop L, and I have a woman under my protection. We are being hunted by an unknown but organized and well-armed group. They have attempted to kill us and abduct the woman with me. Her name is Susanna Stutzman from Treue, Pennsylvania. We are in imminent danger."

A blue van pulled into the parking lot next, and Susanna turned to look at the same time that he did.

"Zeke—"

"I see them," he said, then into the phone he added, "They're here. We know from experience that they are armed and dangerous. We need backup now. Our lives depend on it. There are civilians present who are in danger." Then he turned to Susanna. "Get into the kitchen—out of sight."

He had one clip—six bullets. It wasn't enough. He turned

to the stunned waitress. She looked younger than he'd first thought. She couldn't be more than twenty-five.

"How many men are in pursuit?" the operator asked.

"I don't know how many. They've been after us ever since an attempted abduction in Treue. We've been two days on the run."

"I've got police and ambulance on the way," the woman said. "Can you give me descriptions of your attackers?"

"Two vehicles here right now—a red SUV, and a blue cargo van. As for the men—" He turned to the waitress. "What's your name?"

"What?" she asked, trembling.

"What's your name?" he asked, softening his tone.

"Wendy."

"Wendy, take this phone, and I want you to tell the operator everything you see. Describe the men that come out of those vehicles—clothes, hair, anything that stands out. Got it?" He passed it over to her, and she began recounting the vehicles and the men.

"Um…this is Wendy." The waitress's voice trembled. "There are some men getting out of a red SUV outside. And…and… I see a blue van, too. Yes… Yes…"

Zeke then turned to the few tables that had guests eating their meals. They were all staring at Zeke and Susanna now, though. Their waitress stood with her now-empty tray at her side, looking ready to bolt. "Folks, I need you to get down and move away from windows and doors," Zeke said, raising his voice. He didn't stop to see if they'd complied, because the door to that blue van opened, and a man he and Susanna both recognized got out, along with a beefy-looking sidekick. He sauntered over to the front door and pulled it open almost lazily.

Zeke felt a hand on his back, and he looked over his

shoulder to see Susanna's ashen face. She hadn't retreated. His heart nearly stopped, and he sent up a silent prayer.

"Wendy, get down," Zeke said, trying to keep his voice low. "Susanna—" He wanted to tell her to get down, to slip away, but it was too late now.

The waitress stifled a sob from behind the counter.

"Two men," she whispered. "A big one and a smaller one…"

"You two gave us quite a chase, didn't you?" the smaller man said, coming inside, his dark eyes trained on Zeke and Susanna. "Okay, well… I'll take her, then. You—" He pulled out a gun and waggled it in Zeke's direction. "You annoyed me a whole lot, but I don't have much use for you. I'll take Susanna, though."

Susanna's hand on his back started to tremble, and he pulled himself up straighter. He knew her name. It stood to reason.

"Daniel Schaber, I presume?" he asked conversationally.

The man's face froze. "It doesn't matter."

That was confirmation. This was the one who was giving orders back at the farm. At least Zeke had a face now to go with the name.

"Why do you want her?" Zeke asked. He was stalling now. They needed to give backup time to arrive, and there was no way he was handing Susanna over.

"What's it to you?" The gun steadied, and Daniel's gaze moved around the diner. There was a woman's shriek and the sound of scrambling.

"You aren't touching her," Zeke said, and he pushed Susanna farther back with his hand.

"Don't make this more complicated than it needs to be," the man replied, his voice low and almost singsong in tone. "You'd be surprised to know I don't really have any beef with you. At the moment. And I don't really want a public shooting. That's messy. That can change, of course. You've been a thorn in my side, but I get it. We both have jobs, right? We're two sides of the same coin."

"No, we're not the same at all," Zeke replied. "Why her? Why her specifically?"

Maybe this man would talk. He was the one in control. He must feel the power of the situation. Sometimes people got careless when they figured they held all the cards.

"Because she's been very naughty. Haven't you, Susanna?" The singsong voice suddenly turned to ice. He cocked his head to one side, that gun still training on Zeke's face. "She comes with me."

"How do you know her name?" Zeke pressed. "How do you know her at all?"

Outside the window, the sliding door on the blue van rolled open. Zeke's gaze flicked over the man's shoulder, and he spotted the pale face of a familiar Mennonite girl. She wavered toward the opening before some unseen hand hauled her back and the door slammed shut again.

His heart thudded to a stop. He knew her—the clothes, the slim build, the face... The Weaverland girl those men had left tied in the greenhouse was in that van. They were moving her.

"I don't have time for this," Daniel sighed.

He waggled the gun and tried to push past Zeke, but Zeke made a grab for his wrist with one hand, and the gun with the other. For a moment, Zeke thought he might succeed and get the gun away, but then it felt like a boulder slammed into his shoulder, knocking him to the ground. He tried to sit up, but none of his muscles responded. The pain took a moment to register, but then he felt it...both the pain, and the sticky wetness spreading over his chest.

The man stepped over him, grabbed Susanna and hauled her out the door in one powerful jerk.

Susanna's scream seared through the fog of his pain, and Zeke saw another man with a gun appear in the door, pointing it around the restaurant. Zeke fought for his breath, battling back the nausea and lightheadedness.

His vision slowly cleared and he rolled his head, trying to look around. The gunman had disappeared.

This is shock from a gunshot wound, he told himself. *You've been shot. You are going into shock.*

But he could already tell that nothing vital had been hit. His heart was still beating, for one, and the pain was coming from his shoulder. Not his chest, not his side, not his torso... Those would all be worse. It was his shoulder, and it hurt an awful lot, but with a little bit of blessing, the shot would be in and out, and there wouldn't be a bullet lodged inside of him.

"He's shot!" Wendy was saying into the phone. "The trooper—he's shot! The man with the gun took the Amish woman... They've got her! One man has a gun, and he's pointing it around, and... The trooper—he's bleeding bad!"

Through the fog of his pain and the shock to his system, all Zeke could do was send up a frantic prayer: *Gott, give me strength...*

Rough hands hauled Susanna across the pavement, her struggles doing absolutely nothing to loosen that iron grip. She fought back, her feet going out from under her, but still he dragged her along, her knees scraping painfully against pavement. The sliding door of the van opened, she was hoisted, and she landed inside in a heap. There were no seats in the back but there were metal rails on the floor where seats used to be, and her knee caught against one with an explosion of pain. The door slammed shut, and another man grabbed her hands and zip-tied them together, then did the same to her ankles, the pain from her knee still shattering her thoughts.

"Gag them, Paul," Daniel Schaber ordered.

"With what?"

"I don't know! Find something!"

The man who was apparently named Paul grabbed at her skirt and tried to tear it. He pulled out a knife and sliced into the fabric.

"Hurry up!"

This seemed to be taking more time than they wanted to take.

"They're fine." He held the knife against Susanna's neck. "Make any noise at all, and I kill you. Got it?"

Susanna nodded mutely, and the blade pulled back. He crawled over her and a center console to the front seat. Her heart thundered in her ears.

Susanna tried to twist around and look around her, and spotted another pale face staring back at her. It was a Mennonite girl—younger than Susanna was, and not familiar. The girl was propped up against the wall, and she looked woozy, a little out of it.

But Susanna's mind was still spinning. Back in the diner, Zeke had been shot. She saw him go down, saw the blood spread on his shirt. Was he alive? Had they killed him? Shock had slammed itself over her emotions, and she knew that deep down she wanted to wail, but her eyes remained dry, and her breath came in shallow gasps. If Zeke was dead… She didn't know what she'd do. He'd said he'd put her life before his, and he'd done just that. But maybe he was still alive… He'd been shot in the middle of a diner, with people around, and a telephone, and help on the way. Maybe he wasn't dead!

Oh, Gott, save Zeke!

And may Gott save her and this other girl.

Her brain wasn't moving fast enough. What plans did these men have for them? Why take them at all?

"Okay, we're good. Let's move," Paul said and as the vehicle lurched forward, Susanna was flung backward, landing hard against her shoulder.

She grimaced against the pain and rolled over to find herself face-to-face with the bleary-looking girl.

"Are you okay?" Susanna whispered.

The girl didn't answer at first, then she licked her lips and whispered back, "Are you a dream?"

"No, I'm as real as you are," Susanna whispered. "We're in the back of a van. We've been abducted."

"I'm… I'm having a hard time waking up…"

They'd given her something. Zeke had mentioned the girl at the farm had been drugged. Susanna could be grateful they hadn't done the same to her, and she tried to sit up again, but another bump tossed her back to the floor of the van. Paul in the passenger seat turned around to look at them and seemed satisfied, facing forward again.

Susanna needed to get this girl alert, if at all possible. If they were going to get out of here alive, this girl needed to have her wits about her.

"What's your name?" Susanna whispered.

"Holly…"

"Holly, I'm Susanna Stutzman. How long have they had you?"

"I don't know… I've been… It's been foggy."

"They doped you up."

"*Yah*. I think so. Someone put a needle in my neck, and then…"

"Okay, well, they didn't dope me up yet. Are you tied? Because they've got me tied up."

"Um… My hands are."

They hadn't bothered to bind up Holly's feet—that was something.

"Okay, we have to get our hands free. Start working on it. I've got my feet and my hands tied up. But we have to get free, okay? Find something to saw at the zip ties, or see if you can work one hand out."

Susanna would have to do the thinking for both of them until whatever they'd given Holly wore off. Susanna's wrists were tied too tightly for her to wriggle anything loose, so she started to rub the plastic cord against one of those metal rails in the floor. The men were hotly debating about something in the front and didn't notice.

As for Holly, she started twisting her hands this way and that—her ties were looser. She just might be able to wriggle one hand out.

Susanna started to pray. It was a deep prayer, a desperate prayer. She prayed for her and Holly stuck in the back of this van with men who had evil in their hearts. She prayed for Zeke bleeding on that diner floor. And she prayed for courage because she knew that before she and Holly escaped this nightmare, they were going to have to face evil. And they'd have to win.

TEN

Zeke tried to push himself up from the tiled floor of Rosie's Diner, but a middle-aged woman pushed him firmly back down. She hovered over him as his brain fog started to lift. The woman was slim, had some gray at her temples and had a no-nonsense look about her that he found surprisingly intimidating. She was like one of his high school teachers who had insisted upon proper manners in her classroom and would reply to nothing but "ma'am." For one unsteady moment, he thought maybe she was that teacher...

"Ma'am?" he said.

"Keep still," she said. She looked to be about his mother's age. The silver streaks in her hair glittered in the sunlight, and he blinked a few times, trying to get his mind back into the game. He was on the floor. He'd been shot. Daniel Schaber had Susanna. Zeke tried to sit up again, and the woman put a hand on his collarbone and easily dropped him back to the ground once more.

"My name is Diane. I'm an ER nurse," she said briskly. "Just be glad I came out for a meal with my sister today. You've been shot, by the way. That pain you feel is from a gunshot wound."

Yah, he knew that. And the pain was growing as his adrenaline wore off. He knew academically what was happening to his body, but it didn't seem to help fight off the symptoms. But he was glad to hear that he had a medical professional leaning over him. What he needed was information.

"How many fingers am I holding up?" she asked. Her face leaned closer, and she held up a hand that blurred for a moment in front of his eyes.

"Two." He blinked as she changed the number of fingers. "Four. Two again."

"Okay, you're doing pretty well," she said. "Your body is going to go into shock, though. It doesn't like having extra holes in it. It prefers to hold on to the blood in its veins. Don't take it personally."

"How bad is it?" he asked. "I need to sit up."

"You need to behave," she retorted. "It's a through-and-through gunshot wound."

"That's good news. I was afraid I might have a bullet inside of me still." That would mean the possibility of infections, septic shock…all sorts of miseries. "Look, you need to let me up."

"I actually don't," she said, looking mildly amused. "An ambulance is on the way. You're losing blood, young man, and quickly."

"I don't have time for any of this!" He caught her hand as she tore his shirt from the wound. "Those men just kidnapped a woman in my care. I saw another girl in that van! The cops are coming, but they aren't here yet and every second counts! Do you understand this? Two women are in that van, and they will either be killed or sold into human trafficking. Do you get that?"

Her confidence faded then, and she looked toward the outside door.

"Help me up," he said.

She put a hand behind his neck to give him some assistance, and Zeke pushed himself painfully to a seated position.

"I know I look Amish," he said. "But I am a Pennsylvania State Police detective. I have my badge in my pocket." He dug into his pocket with his good hand and pulled out the badge. "I need to go after them. I promise you I will let the people who haven't been shot take over the minute they arrive. But right now, two women could end up dead if I don't go after them!"

"If you keep bleeding like that, you'll just pass out. Or die," she pointed out. "You aren't going to do a bit of good if you end up unconscious. It isn't about toughness. I've seen cops who are plenty tough pass out into a puddle on the floor from blood loss. You can't 'mind over matter' this."

His heart sank. If she decided to hold him down, she'd succeed. He didn't have the strength to fight her off. But Susanna was out there with that other girl, in the hands of monsters who would do horrible things to them if he didn't stop them first.

"I get that," he said, trying to sound as calm as possible. "I'm hurt. But I've got some strength in me if you'd just help me get bandaged up enough to go after them. Please."

She met his gaze for a moment, and she seemed to be looking for something there. Then she nodded, stood up then and looked around herself. "I need two small towels and a long strip of cloth! Now!"

He breathed a sigh of relief. "Thank you."

Someone seemed to comply with the nurse's orders, because the materials arrived a moment later, and she bent down again and started working on a tight compress. She placed folded towels on either side of his shoulder, pressed hard into his wounds, and tied them with the strip of cloth that she expertly wrapped around his torso and shoulder.

She got onto one side of him, and another patron came to the other side and they helped him to his feet. *Yah*, he could do this.

"I need a vehicle," he said. "We came here on foot."

"You can use mine, but I'm coming with you," she said, pulling out a set of keys as they moved toward the door.

"Diane, I cannot guarantee your safety," he said.

"I can't guarantee yours, either, Detective, but here's the deal. You might be bandaged up, but you are still bleeding. When you do drop, you're going to need me."

He could argue, or they could get moving. This whole situation was already wildly out of control.

"Diane!" another woman gasped. "What are you doing?"

"What needs to be done!" she snapped. This must be the sister she was having lunch with. She turned back to Zeke. "Let's go!"

"Fine," he said. "But I'm driving, and if I tell you to get down, you do it, okay?"

"Deal."

The sister threw up her hands, and Zeke couldn't help but smile as Diane rolled her eyes.

"She's always been the dramatic one," she said.

He had a feeling that if he wasn't already reeling from a gunshot wound, he'd find that darkly funny. They headed out to the vehicle, and he got into the driver's seat. There was a cake box on the back seat, and Diane grabbed a pile of dry cleaning from the passenger seat and threw it into the back, then did up her seat belt. She was dialing her phone at the same time, and she put it on speaker.

"Birthday plans?" he asked.

"My sister's." Diane winced. "I'll make it up to her. Who is the woman that man took?"

The 911 operator picked up, and Diane started explaining the situation in short, clipped sentences. He wasn't paying attention to her, though. Zeke painfully pulled on his own seat belt, and Diane leaned over and clicked it into place for him. Maybe he wasn't quite as good to go as he'd thought. It didn't matter.

"We're heading west on Granger Road," Diane said. "He's still bleeding, and there are two abducted girls in the van. We need the cavalry. Everything you've got! Ambulance, police…give us some fire engines! We need everything!"

"Do you know the abducted women?" the operator asked.

"I know one—Susanna Stuzman," Zeke said, raising his voice to be heard. He pulled out of the parking space and headed for the road. "She's an Amish woman who was targeted by some kind of criminal group. I got in the way of an attempt to abduct her, and they've been after her ever since." He pulled into traffic. "That guy let me go and he took her. That's incredibly worrisome."

Daniel Schaber had let go of a trooper in order to take Susanna. Most criminal types would love to get their hands on a cop—for revenge, to bargain later—but Daniel hadn't bothered. Clearly he didn't intend to get caught, and his focus on Susanna was terrifying.

"Is she a friend? Girlfriend? Wife?" Diane asked.

"No, she's just a civilian." But the words felt like a lie coming out of his mouth. She was just a civilian he'd stepped in to help. He hadn't known her before this. But he did care a whole lot about getting her back. In the last couple of days together she'd become more than a civilian he was protecting.

And that wasn't right, either. He needed to hold those feelings back. But he could tangle with his emotional issues later.

"The driver of the van is named Daniel Schaber," Zeke added, loud enough for the operator to hear. "That's important. He's leading some sort of human trafficking ring. I've got his blood on a handkerchief in my pocket. Susanna bit him when he tried to abduct her the first time two days ago. Not sure how contaminated it is now, but there's definitely DNA to work with."

Zeke stepped on the gas and was pleased with the pep that this particular vehicle had. He leaned forward to see better out the side mirrors and overtook two smaller cars at once, then whipped back in front of them.

A siren would make this a whole lot easier, but then it would also alert the bad guys that he was closing in.

"Are you a Christian, Diane?" he asked.

"Yes."

"Good," he said. "I need you to start praying."

"Already there, sport," she replied with a wry little chuckle.

"Are you regretting coming along?" he asked.

"Not one bit," she said. "You remind me of my son. If he were in trouble, I'd hope that someone would step in and keep him alive."

"You think you're going to keep me alive?" he asked with a wry smile.

"I'm sure going to try!" she retorted, then she put her hands on the dash to brace herself. "That light's red!"

He took a quick look at traffic, whipped around a plumber's truck and carried on out of town. Up ahead through the falling rain he saw the receding back of a blue van ahead of a few other vehicles. He'd made the right choice in the direction he'd come at the very least.

"Here's hoping we attract some police pursuit," he said, and he pushed the pedal down to the floor. Then he raised his voice for the operator on the phone. "We're on Graber, and just crossed Vermillion Drive, heading west."

"Police and ambulance are on their way," the operator said. "There are some road closures with fallen trees, and one tipped semi, but they are on their way. Bad timing. Hang in there."

A tipped semi, too? At least he was on their tail!

Diane grabbed hold of the handle above her door, and he could see her stomping on an imaginary brake in the corner of his vision.

"How long have you been an ER nurse?" he asked.

"Fifteen years—" She gasped, and he swerved around another car.

"Okay, well, I've been a cop for a decade," he said. "You know how in an emergency room you know exactly what to do?" He leaned forward again to check his mirrors and whipped past another intersection without slowing and overtook a sedan. "By the time the doctors get to your patient, you know exactly what the doctors need to do, too, right?"

"Yes…"

"Good, well, that's how I am with my job. I know what I'm doing," he said. "So I'm going to need you to do what I say the minute I say it. I don't want you getting hurt, either."

"Okay. I will."

But she still looked freaked out. He needed to get her back into her emergency instincts again, because then she'd be reacting with the logical part of her brain and that sharp, dark humor of hers.

"What does your son do?" he asked.

"He's a paramedic."

"Hey, nicely done!" He shot her what he hoped was a smile. "Hold on…"

There was one more vehicle between them and an oncoming truck. He had a split second to make his decision, and he was about to pull out and overtake the car in front of them, but he changed his mind. His reaction time wasn't going to be as fast—not with a gunshot wound.

He sighed, and slowed, waiting as the truck rushed past before he pulled out again and overtook the slower vehicle in front of them. Now it was just road between them and that blue van. The rain was starting to slow down, and the windshield wipers started to squeak against the windshield, so he slowed them down, too.

"So you and your son are both used to dealing with emergencies, blood, life and death…all the hard stuff," he said.

"Yes, I guess we are."

"You're going to need that today," he said. "I'm not your son, okay? Your son is safe. I'm your potential patient. And I need you to be calm and fast with everything you do. This isn't personal for you, right? I'm just some stubborn cop who wouldn't stay on the floor where he probably belonged."

"Right." Her voice was steadier now. "Not personal."

"If we were in the ER, you'd be the boss of your domain. Get back into that headspace."

"I'm there." Her voice was firm, controlled. Good.

"Now, I'm about to rear-end this vehicle and enrage

some very bad people. If that back door opens, you duck down and get your head behind the dash, got it?"

"What about you?" she asked.

"I'll worry about me. Now get ready—"

He stepped on the gas once more and came up fast behind the van. There was a crunch, and a surge of agony as he was pushed forward against his seat belt. Just the jolt was enough to make his eyes water. The van swerved, and he braked, staying close behind it.

Susanna was in there, and he could only pray that she was still in one piece. But they had a quota of women to bring to the black market at work in Pennsylvania, and he could only hope they didn't want to waste that. So he had to believe that she was still alive.

She *had* to be alive.

"It's me, Susanna," he whispered, and he sped up, keeping close behind the vehicle until he could nudge it again.

"Gun!" Diane barked, and she ducked down.

He swerved left, staying out of that gun's reach. Zeke was stirring the hornets' nest and angering some very bad men.

"Hold on," he said with a grimace.

Angry men might be dangerous, but they also wouldn't be thinking quite so rationally, either. And Zeke was going to use that to his advantage.

Susanna sawed at the plastic cord around her wrists with all of her strength. It bit into her flesh as she dug it into the metal rail, but it was working. Her wrists were raw and her skin was cut, but she was getting through the plastic. If she and Holly were still bound when this van stopped, they were dead. Or perhaps there would be a future worse than death waiting for them—sold into some horrific slavery, kept submissive with drugs.

Gott, save us! Please save us!

She'd seen just how helpless Holly had been before those drugs wore off, and it was only by the grace of Gott that they wore off when they did. That could not be happenstance. It could not be. Gott was merciful and protected his own. She would cling to that.

"Where did you come from?" Holly whispered.

"I was dragged out of a diner…in Felder."

"With people around?" she gasped.

"*Yah*, broad daylight. Where did you come from?"

"I was walking home from my sister's place… I don't remember much. I thought Shawn was my friend. They grabbed me, and put a needle in my neck. That's all I remember. It's foggy after that."

"Shawn?"

"*Yah*."

She knew that name—her cousin had told her countless times about the wonderful Shawn who loved her so dearly.

Susanna looked toward the driver—Daniel Schaber—and his partner in the front seat. Paul something… They looked occupied with their problems up there—thankfully. "Shawn Neufeld?"

"You know him?"

Susanna's heart thundered to a stop. "Is Shawn one of those men?"

She nodded toward the front seat. "He's the driver." Tears welled in Holly's eyes. "I don't know why he's doing this to me! He was my friend."

And suddenly it all slammed together in Susanna's mind. There was no heartbroken boyfriend Shawn Neufeld out there, mourning the loss of Hannah. There was only Daniel Schaber, a criminal who knew how to gain a woman's trust. Her cousin had fallen in love with a monster!

"Who is that following us?" Paul barked. "Speed up!"

"I'm going as fast as this garbage heap will go!"

"Can you see who it is?"

"No… Wait… No, it can't be… It's the guy I shot!"

The vehicle swerved, and Susanna sawed faster, her heartbeat pattering hard at the base of her throat. Was it possible? Was it Zeke back there?

"It's not the guy you shot."

"I think it is!"

"How did he walk away from a point-blank shot to the chest? It is not him!"

Susanna was almost through the zip tie when something smashed into the van from behind and flung her forward, the cord snapping. Her feet were still bound, although her hands were now free. Holly had one of her hands almost free from her own zip ties, her wrists and the top of the hand she was working free scraped raw.

"I think help is behind us," Susanna whispered. "Someone is chasing the van."

Holly's eyes glittered with hope. "Police?"

Susanna nodded. "I think so. I think it's my…my friend."

Zeke. More than her friend right now. This race for their lives had changed things between them quickly. The very thought of him filled her heart with warmth and hope.

The wiry man in the passenger seat started to turn around to look at them, and Susanna immediately pressed her wrists together. He was distracted, though, and didn't seem to notice the missing zip ties. He pulled out a gun.

"Shoot him!" Daniel's voice exploded through the van.

Paul leaned out of her view, and Susanna started to saw at the plastic cords around her ankles as fast as she could.

"I'm free." Holly's hand came out of the restraint, and she rubbed at her chafed wrists.

"Help me," Susanna whispered.

Holly crawled over to where Susanna sat, adding her own strength to sawing through the plastic. The sound of a gunshot shattered the air, then another. Holly and Susanna both froze.

"Hurry!" Susannah whispered, and Holly leaned into the work.

There was another shuddering thump from the back of the van, and both women fell forward again, but this time, Susanna found herself next to a sharp metal protuberance from the floor, at the perfect angle.

Danke, Gott!

She shoved the frayed plastic against the sharp metal and with a few hard swipes, it cut clean through. She was free!

"Where do we go?" Holly whispered. "Can we get out the back door?"

Another spattering of gunfire tore through the air, and the van rocked from side to side, sending Susanna against the wall. She had to come up with a plan. Right now the van was speeding too fast to throw themselves out the back door. But they couldn't just wait for the van to stop. She knew the minute those men found out she and Holly had gotten loose from their bindings, there would be brutal consequences.

"Whatever we do, it had better be fast!" Susanna whispered.

"I can't shoot him out the window," Paul said. "Hold on—I've got an idea."

The man came over the back of the seat, and his small, squinty eyes landed on the cut zip ties on the dirty floor of the van.

"What the—" A meaty hand shot out and he caught Susanna by the hair, hauling her toward him. She felt a clump of hair pull free of her scalp with a blinding rip of pain, and she reached up, clawing at the hand that tore at her hair.

"How'd you get loose?" he snarled, foul breath enveloping her, and he slammed her face into the side of the van. Blood misted over her vision, and black spots danced in front of her eyes. She blinked her vision back into focus just as he grabbed Holly by the throat and punched her full in the face with the butt of his gun. The slim woman crumpled into a heap, and Susanna couldn't take her eyes off the blood pooling on the dirty floor, dribbling out of Holly's mouth and nose.

"Hey, don't manhandle the merchandise," Daniel snapped. "I want top dollar for them."

These men intended to sell them. They'd be kept alive for evil intents that Susanna was terrified to even form in her mind. If they didn't escape, they were going to wish they'd died in this van.

Paul crawled over her and pushed at a big lever that would release the door. She lay there, afraid to move, watching the man brace himself.

She would not be sold into slavery to die at the hands of monsters. She would not, that she vowed. She would fight to survive, and if she died in that fight, it was far better than suffering through a brutal lifetime of whatever these men had in mind.

"Holly!" Susanna whispered, crawling painfully over to where the other girl lay motionless. Her head ached, and the movement sent excruciating pain throbbing into her temples.

From the front seat Daniel barked, "What are you doing back there?"

"The heifers got loose," Paul spat out.

"What?"

The van swerved again as Daniel turned to look back, and Susanna dropped limp and let her eyes fall shut. She heard the back door open, the rush of air and the echo of gunshots.

She opened her eyes again. Daniel was facing the road again, and she pushed herself up to her hands and knees. Holly started to stir, and Susanna shook her shoulder.

"Wake up!" she whispered. "Shh… Wake up!"

Holly moaned, and Susanna put her hand gently over her lips. "Shh… Open your eyes."

Holly struggled to open them, and Susanna braced herself as the van swerved once more and there was another gunshot.

"Daniel, cut it out! Keep the van straight," the big man bellowed, bracing himself against the doorframe. The heavy back door swung on its hinges, and Susanna's heart caught in her throat.

The man was hovering in the open doorway, his gun arm extended as he unloaded a spray of bullets into the road behind them.

And suddenly, Susanna saw the choice in front of her. There was a way to rid themselves of one of these thugs, but it might kill the man. In fact, it would very likely kill him. If she was to escape, Susanna might be forced to take a life.

The history lessons from their Anabaptist roots swept through her mind—people who had been willing to face death themselves rather than take another life. People who had faced martyrdom rather than commit murder, even in self-defense. Better people than Susanna, apparently.

Paul pulled out another clip Johd reloaded his gun, still not turning around. Apparently, he thought they were both too badly beaten to move, but he had sorely miscalculated Susanna's desire to live.

Gott, what do I do?

She saw an exit—blocked with an off-balance criminal who was trying to kill the only help they had coming for them.

Zeke. Her heart swelled with tenderness. Zeke who was coming for her. Zeke who would put his own life before hers. Well, she couldn't sit here and let him die, either.

The thunder of gunshots echoed through the van interior, and Susanna pushed herself to her feet and crept forward.

Gott, have mercy on me, she prayed in her heart. *Don't let him die. I don't want to take a life!*

The van went over a bump, and she staggered backward, falling back onto her rump, just as Paul turned.

"What are you doing?" he roared, grabbing her by the hair once more. Susanna struggled against his grip, digging her nails into his hand. She'd bite him if she could just get the right angle. She managed to get his pinky finger loose and she pulled back with all her strength. There was a pop, and he cried out, staggered, and with a shout, fell backward out of the van and disappeared with a bile-rising thud.

Her heart nearly stopped. What had just happened? Tires screeched, and the door swung on those squeaky hinges.

Susanna looked out the back of the van to see a green SUV go sailing off the road into a ditch and a lumpy body lying in the middle of the road, sprawled right on top of the dotted yellow line separating them. She thought she saw him move—did he move?

"Paul!" Daniel shouted.

The van started to slow. Did Daniel know the fate of his partner yet? Susanna wasn't sure, but they could not afford to wait to find out. She pushed herself to her feet just as Holly struggled to hers. Blood smeared across the tender flesh of Holly's chin and neck, and dried rust-colored blood crusted over her hand.

"We have to jump," Susanna said, reaching for Holly's hand.

"We can't—"

"I'm not leaving you here!" Susanna said. "Holly, we jump or we get sold! Did you hear them? They're selling us! We have to jump! I'm not leaving you, but I'm not staying, either!"

Holly took a step forward, and they crouched at the bumper of the van, the back door swinging and the air whistling past their ears. The SUV was far behind now, and Susanna watched the ditch whip past in a green blur. She'd rather land in weeds and water than on the cement.

"On three—" Susanna clutched Holly's hand.

"Gott, protect us…" Holly breathed.

"One, two…" The van slowed, and Susanna rose to her feet, one hand on the side of the doorframe and the other clasping Holly's.

"Paul!" And then Daniel let loose with a string of foul curses that made a shudder run down her spine.

It was now or never. "Three!"

And they leaped.

ELEVEN

Susanna hit the grass by the side of the road and rolled, her shoulder jarring painfully. She heard Holly land a heartbeat later, and for what felt like an eternity, Susanna struggled to pull air back into her lungs. Her body felt like it was moving in slow motion as she pushed herself up onto her hands and knees. Everything hurt—her joints, her knees where gravel was digging into her skin, her hips… Even sucking breath into her lungs felt like tearing flesh. Black spots spun in front of her eyes.

"Holly," she croaked. She forced her eyes open and looked around for her friend. This stretch of highway was narrow and winding, and there were trees on either side of the road. Holly lay a yard away on the gravel shoulder of the road. Her arm was at a strange angle, and her hair that had come loose from what was left of her bun concealed half of her white face. But that arm had Susanna's attention— at first she couldn't quite say what was wrong with it, but then she pinpointed the break. It was the wrist—her hand at a disturbing angle, and a bulge in her forearm right above the wrist. Susanna's stomach heaved. It was badly broken.

"Holly!" Her mind was catching up now, and she crawled over to the young woman's side. "Holly, we have to move!"

Holly's eyes looked glassy from pain, and Susanna

grabbed her good arm and pulled her up. She let out a cry that made Susanna instinctively release her.

"You have to move or we die!" Susanna begged. "I know it hurts, but we have to move!"

Holly tried again, and then retched onto the ground, emptying what little was inside her stomach. Then with a grimace, she pulled her wounded arm against her body, her breath coming in shuddering gasps, and Susanna helped her to her feet. She tugged her along with her over the ditch and into the trees on the side of the road. Holly stumbled and her knees looked ready to give out on her, but Susanna couldn't leave her behind. She had a blurry sense of what those men would do with Holly if they got their hands on her again, and she knew this current agony was nothing compared to the life waiting for her if they sold her for other men's evil desires.

The van stopped ahead on the road and then the white reverse lights came on and the vehicle started to back up.

"Hurry!" Susanna gasped. "He's coming!"

They pushed farther into the undergrowth, and Susanna pulled the girl with her behind a dense group of trees. Briars scratched at her ankles, and twigs swiped at her torn dress. Her breath was coming in gasps, and Holly trembled next to her. The leafy brush at the base of the trees was dense enough that Susanna thought it might obscure them at the very least.

Susanna paused, listening. She didn't hear anything— no rumbling engine, no voices… She held her breath and looked back through the trees toward the road. The blue van was parked at the side of the road. He was here somewhere. She could feel it like a shiver on the back of her neck. Daniel Schaber wasn't letting them go.

And then she heard the crunch and splinter of footsteps moving through dry underbrush.

"Come out, come out, wherever you are!" Daniel sang out in a soft voice. "I'll find you. You know I will. You might as well just come out now."

Holly wavered on her feet, and Susanna grimaced as she tightened her grip around the girl's waist to hold her upright.

"I will punish you when I find you, Susanna," he called out in that same eerie voice. "You have taken my property, and I don't like that. When people mess with my merchandise, they die. You do realize that, don't you? You've also killed one of my men, and that annoys me, too."

Susanna squeezed her eyes shut, trying to control her own breathing that sounded too loud in her own ears. Had she killed that man? Was she responsible for a man's death? She heard a car pass, and Susanna wondered if they'd call 911.

"I liked Paul," Daniel went on as his boots crunched along, coming closer in one moment, and then farther away in the next. She couldn't tell where he was. "He was a decent lackey, and you crushed his skull on a highway. Honestly, I didn't think you had it in you. You're tougher than Hannah was."

Susanna's heart nearly stopped as grief for her cousin welled up inside of her. Poor Hannah—her cousin who had trusted the wrong man, who loved the wrong man. She'd thought that Shawn—Daniel—would give her the romance she longed for. She'd trusted him. And it had led to her death.

Holly's knees buckled and she let out a soft moan as she sank down to the ground. It wasn't much noise, but it seemed that it was enough because those steps suddenly turned and came crashing in their direction. And then Daniel appeared, a gun in his right hand, hanging comfortably at his side. When he spotted them, a slow smile spread over his face.

"Gotcha," he said softly.

Susanna's heart hammered in her throat, and she carefully pulled her arm free of her friend, who sat at the base of the tree. Daniel walked around to get a better look at her, and he made a soft tutting sound.

"You damaged my merchandise, Susanna. I warned you about that."

"She's not merchandise!" Susanna snapped.

"She most certainly is. And so are you. You look like you're in better shape than she is, though." He slowly shook his head. "She's worth very little like that. My clients want to break a woman themselves, not have her delivered like… that." He waved the gun toward Holly. "And I was very careful with her until you came along. Do you see what you've done?"

"She needs a doctor," Susanna said feebly.

He laughed. "And you think I'll take her to one?"

Nee, she didn't think that. The man's insane logic was twisting all over the place and she was having trouble following it.

"Let me explain how this works," he said. "If I take her to a doctor, then there will be questions asked. We can't have that. I'm…staying under the radar, so to speak. Do you understand what that means?"

She nodded numbly.

"Good. I thought you might not, seeing as you don't know anything about technology." He laughed as if it were a personal joke, and then sobered immediately. "If my merchandise gets damaged, I simply have to get rid of it."

Daniel lifted the gun and Susanna dove in front of Holly. "Don't kill her!"

"Why not? She's worthless!"

"She's not!" Susanna shouted. "She's not! Is that what happened to Hannah? Did she get hurt and you killed her?"

Except there had been no sign of injury, besides the gunshot wound. She remembered that now. Just a shot in the head—that was all. A confusing execution.

"Ah…" Daniel's expression smoothed. "Your cousin. Of course. That was unavoidable."

"What happened to her?" Susanna demanded. "You called yourself Shawn Neufeld, didn't you? It's a name you've used before."

He didn't answer, eyes narrowing.

"She loved you, you know!" Susanna pressed. "She did! She told me how you'd go visit her and take her out shopping. You listened to her talk for hours. You took so much time getting her trust…"

Just to kidnap her? Just to sell her? Susanna sucked in a wavering breath. He'd taken so much time with one girl, when he could have abducted her at any point. Why?

"What happened to her?" she pleaded.

"I wasn't going to sell Hannah," Daniel said. "I was going to keep her for myself, but she was a fighter. Amish girls are supposed to be sweet and submissive, but she wouldn't know her place. She kept nagging and nagging… But you would know all about that, wouldn't you? She was writing you letters. I found one."

Nagging? That sounded nothing like Hannah. She hadn't been the submissive type, but she hadn't been a nag, either.

"What did she fight against?" Susanna stepped away from Holly. There was a clearer patch a few feet away. And Daniel couldn't shoot both her and Holly at once. If she could just get a little farther away…

"I told her to never ask about my business," he said darkly. "But she kept asking. She kept nagging, and arguing that my colleagues were bad men. She kept putting her nose into my work. That's bad behavior, you know. You know that, don't you? But she was telling you about my work—I know that. She filled pages of chicken scratch with the things she saw."

That was what she'd written in the last letter—she'd seen something!

"Ironically, you're right," Susanna said. "Amish girls don't do that with their men. They let men's business be. But if Hannah were a meeker woman, she would never have left her parents' house. You couldn't have both, Daniel. She could either be meek and submissive and never be yours, or be daring enough to run away with you and have some strong opinions of her own."

What did Hannah see?

Susanna was baiting him now, distracting him with thoughts of Hannah while she eyed that gap in the trees behind him.

"I suppose." Daniel pursed his lips, and she took another step to the side. "Maybe I was being silly, then. Maybe love made me blind."

Love? Daniel Schaber had no idea what love was!

"So how did she die, then?" Susanna pressed. Another step. And another. A twig snapped under her shoe.

"She found one of my…pieces of merchandise." He shook his head sadly. "I think she was jealous."

"Why do you think that?"

"She demanded that I let her go. She said she'd seen her in the shed. I found the letter she tried to mail, and then she tried to free my property. I had no choice. She had to be stopped. She wouldn't see reason."

So it was Daniel who'd shot her cousin, but somehow it made Susanna feel a little bit better to understand the circumstances. Hannah had been trying to save a girl. She'd tried to tell Susanna about it in a letter, too. She'd died a hero.

"So you came after me—thinking I knew," she said.

"Didn't you?" He shook his head slowly. "You are a lying little minx, aren't you? Lies upon lies. Just like Hannah."

Daniel really did think her cousin had told her something incriminating, it seemed.

"I'm not lying." She couldn't help the tremor in her voice.

"I saw what she said in that letter. She told you all about the girl in the shed, and she'd snooped around and found some guns, too. Good girls don't snoop. She sealed your fate herself."

"Did you feel anything at all when you killed her?" Susanna asked, stepping farther toward that clearing. "Did she mean anything to you?"

"I mourned her!" Daniel roared. "I mourned the woman she should have been, the nagging brat! If she'd just been a little bit sweeter, she'd still be alive!"

But Hannah had laid her own life down for another. Surely Gott above had seen her sacrifice and would reward her in eternity. Tears misted her eyes, and she blinked them back. She took another step, and she was out of the brush.

"She loved you," Susanna whispered. "She was wrong, of course. You're a monster. But I hope you never forgive yourself for what you've done. I hope it eats you up."

Anger darkened the man's eyes. "It's like you want to die."

Did she? She preferred a bullet to the brutal life of slavery he had planned for her. But her fixation was not on dying—it was on the road behind them. Another car passed. She had a straight run for that road…

One moment she felt weighted to the spot, and the next, she took off at a sprint. Daniel barked out a curse, and she felt his fingers slip off her shoulder as she flew past him. But he was fast, too, and as she reached the tree line, she felt an iron grip on her hair, and she was jolted to a stop. Her teeth clicked together, and she tasted blood in her mouth. An arm slammed against her throat and he hauled her back. But she wasn't going to give up without a fight, either, and she kicked and writhed, and managed to get her chin down far enough to sink her teeth into that salty-tasting arm.

He shouted out another curse and released her. She could taste copper in her mouth—his blood this time—and she tried to take off again, but her foot caught on a root and she fell flat onto her face. A strong arm caught her ankle, and she felt herself being pulled backward, her dress catching and tangling up around her. She flipped herself over onto her back and kicked out with her one free foot.

He bellowed when she caught his finger with one hard kick and she heard an ugly snap. She'd broken his finger— she could see the odd angle that it hung away from his hand.

Daniel let go of her for a split second, then snatched the front of her dress and pulled her upward to meet the butt of his gun in her face. Everything spun and almost went black. Pain exploded across the bridge of her nose, but then she heard a voice that pierced through the pain and nausea.

"Let go of her. Now."

She blinked her eyes open as Daniel spun her around and she felt the cold, hard metal of a gun pressing into her temple. Her head was pushed to the side with the pressure of the weapon, and she sucked in a cautious breath as her eyes focused on the man standing at the tree line, his own gun held out in front of him.

Zeke was bloody, and it looked like someone had bandaged him up. But he was upright, and his gaze flicked to meet hers for just a moment before his attention locked back onto Daniel.

"I said to let go of her," Zeke repeated. "Now."

* * *

Zeke felt his hand tremble and he squeezed his gun a little harder to keep it under control. His shoulder was screaming with pain holding his gun up like this, but if he relaxed, even for a moment, he wasn't sure he'd be able to raise his arm again.

And backup wasn't here yet. But he could hear the sirens. They were close.

When that man had come flying out the back of the van, he'd bounced off the hood of the SUV, sending them into the ditch. Zeke hadn't been able to get the vehicle out again. So he told Diane to stay with it and to point emergency personnel in the right direction when they did eventually arrive.

And Zeke had set out on foot. He'd meant to be jogging, but he feared it was more of a staggering walk in reality. All the same, it was his panicked, last-ditch effort. It appeared to be the right choice, though, because the van had eventually stopped, and he passed by the moaning heap that was the man who'd gone soaring out the back of the van. He didn't even slow to check on him. The man was obviously alive based on the groans emanating from him but he wasn't going anywhere, and Zeke's priority was Susanna and the other girl, not their kidnappers. With that slow, warm, seeping feeling running down his side, he knew he didn't have a lot of time, either.

And then he'd heard the voices and Susanna's scream and grunts of a fight. He'd bolted across the ditch and spotted her fighting like a wet cat. He'd never been more impressed in his life!

But he couldn't get a clear shot at Daniel. Trees blocked his view until he could get close enough. Now, seeing that man with a gun smash in Susanna's face, he felt all the rage boil up inside of him until his injury no longer mattered.

He'd get her free, or he'd die trying. And if he died, he was taking that monster with him.

Daniel held Susanna in front of him like a shield, ducking his own face behind her head. On a better day—one with less blood loss perhaps—he would have been able to get a head shot in, but there was no way he'd make that shot today. He'd either miss completely or kill Susanna.

"Let her go," Zeke said.

Daniel laughed. "That would be very stupid on my part, wouldn't it?"

"What's your plan?" Zeke asked.

"Kill you."

"That might be easier said than done."

"That's cute. Have you looked in a mirror lately? I shot you. You're bleeding out."

Daniel wasn't wrong. Zeke could feel his mind getting foggy, and his hand started to tremble again. The pain from the shot through his shoulder was an intense throb, but it was starting to feel less invasive. Was that shock, or blood loss? He wasn't sure. Diane would probably know. Thank God she was safe with the vehicle in the ditch.

"I'm also here," Zeke said. "If you meant to kill me back at the diner, it didn't work."

God had gotten him this far, and that meant more than a man like Daniel could possibly comprehend.

Zeke took a step closer, and Daniel backed up, dragging Susanna with him.

"Are you okay, Susanna?" Zeke asked.

"I'm okay—" she called back, her voice cutting off when the gun pressed harder against her head.

"You could just drop her and fight me," Zeke said. "It looks like she did quite a number on you, too."

"You take me for an idiot? I'm not letting her go."

"Why the fixation on her?" Zeke asked, keeping his voice conversational.

"You tell me!" Daniel barked out. "You're here, bleeding like a stuck pig and very likely going to die, all for her."

"You're the one who pulled me into this when you tried to kidnap her. I'm sorry—I'm a man who takes human trafficking personally. So is that it—you want to sell her?"

"I do have a quota to fill."

"I'd like to hear about that quota," he said.

"You probably would."

"Who are you selling women to?"

"Private parties."

"How much do they pay?" He was starting to see that this would be a pretty expensive service—abducted women to private parties. Very likely wealthy men with sickening tastes. That wasn't a poor creep's pastime.

"Why, you want in?" Daniel laughed softly, and Zeke's stomach churned. This man was disgusting.

"They must pay well," Zeke said. "I've seen your array of toys."

Daniel laughed softly. "They are impressive. But you're trying to distract me."

"Maybe," Zeke agreed. "You're doing the same. Your lackey isn't coming to help you. He's in bad shape on the highway."

He saw the horror well up in Susanna's eyes, and he realized in a rush that she was probably the one who'd pushed him out of the van.

"He's alive, though," he added for her benefit. "In a lot of pain, moaning and groaning, but alive."

A nerve twitched at the side of Daniel's cheek. So he was irritating him. Good. He wouldn't stay rational, then. Mistakes happened when men got riled up.

"Were you expecting him to come back and surprise me?" Zeke asked.

"No, I'm waiting for you to lose more blood," Daniel replied, and a sinister smile touched his lips. "I don't think I have to wait much longer."

Zeke truly hated that the man had a point. He was losing blood at a pretty good rate now, his whole side feeling slick from the wound in his shoulder. If he'd been interested in self-preservation, he would have stayed on the ground in the diner and let medical professionals take care of him. But this wasn't about him. It was about getting Susanna free—whatever the cost.

"Well, keep wasting time, then, because I've got backup coming," Zeke said. "Any minute now."

Susanna wriggled then, twisting in the man's grip and jerking to get free of his grasp. Daniel tightened his hold around her neck, and Susanna's face turned red as her breath was cut off. Her eyes bulged, and her lips turned purple then blue, her resistance fading. Daniel was going to strangle her! As she scraped at his arm with weakening fingers, her mouth open, Zeke's heart hammered hard against his rib cage. If he had a little more strength, he might take a run at the man, but in this condition he wouldn't make it across the clearing.

Zeke took a step closer, though—he could do that much. Daniel pulled the gun away from her head and fired a shot at Zeke. He missed. How many bullets did Daniel have in that magazine? Ten? Less? Zeke only had six bullets, and they needed to count.

"If she passes out, she's going to drop. You won't be able to hold up her dead weight, and it's going to expose your entire body. Then I will shoot you," Zeke said. "Just so you know."

Daniel loosened his grip across her neck and Susanna exhaled a sputtering, ragged breath. Zeke felt his own breath come easier as the red seeped out of her face again. Her terrified gaze rose then, and met his.

He couldn't explain how, but he could see that she'd not only heard his words, but she'd understood his hint. His own strength was waning, and his trembling hand started to shake in earnest. His arms felt like lead, and the trees around him had started a slow, tilted spin. He was about to pass out.

And then Susanna jumped up and shot her legs straight out, dropping to the ground in one sliding movement. Daniel's eyes widened in momentary shock, but the action left his torso completely exposed—just as Zeke had predicted.

In that split second before Daniel could react, Zeke squeezed the trigger three times, and Daniel fell backward. Then Zeke felt his knees give out, and he crumpled to the ground.

The trees above him seemed to be spinning in a slow circle around him, and his stomach heaved, wanting to empty itself, as if he even had the strength. The ache in his shoulder felt far away now—he could feel it like a mountain of pounding pain, but he felt like he was walking away from that mountain, and it was a strange relief to be doing so.

But far away—or was it close by? He couldn't tell anymore—he heard the whoop of approaching police sirens mingled with the wail of an ambulance.

And everything went black.

TWELVE

Susanna lay on the ground, the gunshots still echoing through the air. Daniel landed with an awful thud behind her, and for a moment she lay there, frozen. Zeke had fallen, too, and she felt trapped between the two men—one she feared, and one she loved. Her throat felt bruised and raw, and every breath burned. Daniel Schaber would have strangled her—she knew that. He would have let her die there, cut off from oxygen and blood flow. She exhaled a shaking breath and forced her body to move. She crawled away from Daniel's supine body, and she started to tremble.

"Zeke?" she whispered hoarsely.

She could hear the stamp of police troopers farther off in the underbrush. They were no longer alone, but Zeke didn't answer.

Susanna could see that Holly had propped herself up against the tree, holding her poor, mangled wrist against her body while her wide eyes followed Susanna's movement.

And Daniel? Was he dead? Susanna turned, unsure if she even wanted to look, but she needed to know before she turned her back on him again. She struggled to her feet and crept closer, watching for movement, but his chest remained still, and his eyes were open, but his pupils were dilated, and his stare was fixed. Dead. That was what it meant. Three round patches of blood were in a triangle pattern over his chest, but the blood wasn't seeping.

She looked toward Zeke, his chest rising and falling in a reassuring rhythm, then back at the gun still in Daniel's hand. She hurried around Daniel's body—somehow afraid to step over him—and kicked the gun from his relaxed grip, sending it bouncing into the underbrush. There—she'd feel better without a loaded weapon at her back. Then she staggered through the trees toward Zeke, who lay in a similar position to Daniel, flat on his back, except he was visibly breathing. His eyelids fluttered.

Police radios chattered somewhere from the direction of the road, and Susanna knelt down next to Zeke, leaning over him carefully. He slowly lifted his hand and tenderly covered hers with his cool fingers. The gentleness of the gesture brought tears to her eyes, and her chin trembled.

"Zeke?" she whispered, swallowing painfully. "Zeke, are you all right?"

"*Yah*," he whispered back. "Right as rain."

Relief flooded through her—he was doing better than Daniel was, and that was all that mattered.

A woman with gray in her hair appeared from the road, eyes wide and darting. She was dressed in jeans and a smart-looking top that was now streaked with rust-colored blood. But Susanna didn't think it was hers—the woman looked fine otherwise, alert and cautious.

"I found them!" the woman shouted, and she hurried in their direction. "Is he alive?"

Tears welled in Susanna's eyes. "*Yah*, but he was shot earlier. He's lost a lot of blood."

Susanna leaned over Zeke's face and his eyes fluttered open. She barely registered that the whooping sirens had stopped.

"That's Diane," Zeke said, his words quiet. "She…came along for the ride."

"I'm a nurse," Diane cut in. "But the ambulance is here, and the police. I'm going to bring them over."

Diane disappeared, and Susanna looked down at the blood-soaked towels covering Zeke's shoulder. His shirt was crimson, and his hand was stained with fresh blood. How much blood had he lost? How had he stood upright long enough to save her? It was astonishing!

"There's an ambulance for you," Susanna said, trying to keep her shaking voice calm.

Zeke moaned and tried to raise himself up and she easily pushed him back down again. "Stop it, Zeke. You're in bad shape. Just lie still."

"I told you I'd come for you," he said.

"And you came… But I'm okay, and you need a doctor very badly—"

"I look worse than I feel," he said softly.

"I doubt that." But she smiled down at him, her eyes stinging with unshed tears.

"The other girl?"

"She's injured, but she'll be okay," Susanna said, looking over her shoulder toward Holly, whose eyes were shut now as she leaned against that tree.

"Daniel Schaber?"

"He's dead."

"Are you sure?" Zeke's eyes opened again, and this time he struggled again to rise.

"*Yah*, I'm sure." She swallowed. "The police will take care of him."

Zeke winced and fell back. "I really wish I could check that for myself."

"Trust me. I kicked the gun away, too."

"That's my girl." His eyes fell shut again, and his face seemed to grow even paler, if that was possible.

"Zeke?" He was silent. "Zeke?"

His breath seemed to be more shallow now, and she looked over him desperately.

"Don't you die on me, Zeke!" she whispered hoarsely, and she looked down at his ashen lips, the mouth that had been so reassuring, so kind, so protective…the lips that had almost kissed her… This man had done more for her in a matter of days than anyone had done for her in her lifetime.

With Zeke, she'd been safe, and he'd been true to his promise—his life before hers. She'd heard the marriage passage read in multiple weddings, *Husbands, love your wives, even as Christ also loved the church, and gave Himself for it,* and those words echoed in her memory as she looked down at this man who truly just poured himself out, every last ounce of strength, his very blood, in order to save her.

How could she ever thank him? How could she ever explain to him the depth of her tenderness and gratitude? In a way she couldn't quite put into words, she was his. And that part of her would always remain his, no matter what happened in the future. Even if she never saw him again.

But she didn't have the words, so she did the one thing that felt like an approximation of those deep feelings, and she lowered her lips over his in a tender kiss. Her first. She'd never kissed a man before, and she wasn't even sure if she'd done it right. But when she pulled back, his eyes opened again and a faint smile touched those ashen lips.

"I can't do much about it now," he said softly, "but just as soon as they put me back together again, I'm going to kiss you properly."

Maybe she'd done it wrong. How was she supposed to know? She suddenly felt a wave of embarrassment.

"That wasn't proper?" she whispered.

"Let's just say I want to be a more active participant." Even on death's door, humor tinged his tone.

The ambulance attendants came crashing through the brush along with two troopers, and she stood up and waved to show them where Zeke was. They came over to where Zeke lay and put the stretcher beside him.

"He was shot in his shoulder," Susanna said. "He's lost a lot of blood."

"Any other injuries that you know of?" the young ambulance attendant asked.

"I don't think so."

"Allergies to medications?"

"I don't know…"

"Blood type?"

"I don't know…"

"We've got all that in his file," a trooper said, and he pressed a button on his radio. "We need the medical file for Detective Zeke Esch STAT."

Susanna knew very little about Zeke, she realized, at least in the practical sense. But she knew his character, and she knew his heart. But even with all of that reassurance to the kind of man he was, he wasn't Amish.

"All right, Zeke, is it? We're going to move you onto the stretcher. In one…two…" And the two young men hoisted him together. "We need you to stay with us. Stay alert. Focus on my voice."

Diane appeared again, watching anxiously as the paramedics carried the stretcher toward the road, but then she hurried briskly over to Susanne's side. A trooper came with her, and squatted down next to Susanna. Diane reached out and gently touched a tender lump on her forehead.

"You're a nurse?" Susanne asked.

"I am." Diane held her cheeks between two cool hands as she looked into her face. "Your nose might be broken. First, though, follow my finger with your eyes."

"I'm not the worst off," Susanna said, trying to take a step back, but Diane was stronger. "There's another girl—"

Diane turned in the direction that Susanna had been looking. She wilted for just a moment, and then straightened.

"Oh my…" she breathed, and she hurried over to Holly's side and bent down. Two more troopers came up and hurried to help Holly, too.

"Miss? Miss? Can you hear me?" Diane asked Holly.

"Her name is Holly," Susanna said. "She was abducted. They put something in her neck earlier to knock her out, but she woke up enough for us to get out of the van. We jumped, and she was badly hurt in the fall."

"I'm seeing a broken wrist here," Diane said, her voice low, controlled and reassuring. "She's in shock." She put a hand on Holly's cheek. "Holly? Holly? I need you to try to open your eyes, sweetie. Okay? Can you open your eyes?"

Holly's eyes blinked open, but she still looked bleary.

"Holly, my name is Diane, and I'm a nurse. We're waiting on another ambulance to arrive." She straightened at the sound of another siren. "That sounds like it there. I'm going to help you, okay? You can trust me. The man who hurt you is dead."

Tears welled up in Holly's eyes and she started to cry softly, hunched over her mangled wrist.

"I know, sweetie, I know," Diane said.

The police were closing in, and two troopers helped to steady Holly while the other trooper gave Susanna a sympathetic look from where he squatted next to her. Another trooper squatted next to Daniel's body.

"Are you okay?" the police officer next to her asked, pulling her attention back to him.

"I'm fine, I think." She felt foggy, and suddenly very tired.

"What's your name?"

She went through the questions—her name, her birth date, where she was from, if anything hurt...

"We're going to get you to a hospital to check you out," the trooper said. "But we're here to help you. I want you to sit down and let a paramedic see to your injuries, okay? We can talk about what happened to you after that. But first, we need to make sure you're okay."

"I don't think I'm badly hurt. I'm okay," Susanna said. Her throat felt raw and sore, though, from where Daniel had crushed her.

"Susanna, just trust us on this one," Diane called from a few yards away.

"Let's get down to the road," the trooper said. "Can you stand?"

Susanna rose to her feet and allowed the trooper to guide her back toward the road, trying not to look at Daniel's body as she passed. When they got to the road, an ambulance was pulling away, sirens blaring, and another had just arrived.

"There's a girl up there who is badly hurt," Susanna said, pointing. "A nurse is with her, but she needs help."

The paramedics gave her a hesitant look, and then two of them headed off with a stretcher in the direction she'd pointed. The third one—a woman—reached up and gingerly touched Susanna's forehead.

"My name is Jeanette," the woman said. "Can you tell me your name?"

She was led to a seat and pressed down into it. Susanna answered the questions as they were posed to her, and the paramedic tore open an IV line and pushed up Susanna's sleeve.

"This will be a pinch, but I'm going to get you hooked up to some fluids."

"I'm okay. It's the other girl, Holly—" Susanna started, and she looked in the direction of the disappearing ambulance taking Zeke to a hospital. The siren's wail flowed over Amish farmland as it carried off the best man Susanna had ever known toward doctors who she prayed could save him.

"The other paramedics are helping her," Jeanette said firmly. "And I'm helping you. Just a pinch now…"

Gott, save Zeke's life! she prayed. *Please save him!*

Zeke's mouth felt like cotton balls, and when he moved his tongue around, even his teeth felt dry. He closed his lips and let some moisture return to his mouth, but it still felt sticky. Where was he? He tried to open his eyes, but the light was blinding and he squeezed them shut again.

"He's waking up."

"Yes, it looks like." Warmth descended over him with a comforting weight. A blanket? It felt nice.

He tried to open his eyes again and had more success this time. He was in a hospital bed, and everything smelled and tasted medicinal, if that made sense. It was like the scent was originating from inside of him. That would be the anesthetic, he reasoned.

"Am I okay now?" he asked, his voice coming out in a croak.

"You are." He knew that voice, and he turned his head to see the chief sitting down next to his bed. "You just got out of surgery, and the doctor says you're doing really well."

"Surgery on what?" he asked, still feeling somewhat bleary.

"Your shoulder. You were shot."

"Right." It was coming back to him now. He'd gone after Susanna and the other girl. "Are they—" The sight of Schaber holding a gun to Susanna's head appeared before him. "Susanna? Is she okay?"

"Both women you rescued from that van are in good shape, all things considered. The young Weaverland Mennonite girl has a broken wrist, a broken nose and jaw and two cracked ribs. She'll take time to heal."

"And Susanna?" he pressed.

"The Amish woman—she's got a cracked cheekbone, and a hairline fracture in her nose. She's got bumps and scrapes, but other than some terrible bruising on her face, she'll be okay."

"And emotionally?"

"Better than the other girl," the chief said quietly. "She's a tough one. She was more worried about you."

"Where is she now?"

"With her aunt and uncle in her home community near Treue. We have troopers doing patrols around their farm."

She was safe and with family. That was very good for her, but his heart still gave an unexpected squeeze. He'd hoped to see her when he woke up. Honestly, he'd hoped to make good on his promise to kiss her.

But looking up at his boss, Zeke would be wise to rethink that course of action. He was a police officer, and she was a civilian he'd protected. Those were lines a cop couldn't cross. But more importantly, she was Amish and he was no longer. Those lines couldn't be crossed, either. He'd had a job to do and he'd done it. This was supposed to be over now. Victim's Services would take over now. She'd be in good hands.

There was a table on the other side of his bed, and on

it were three different vases of flowers, a big card with a bunch of signatures he could just see from the way it was sitting, and a small teddy bear wearing an old-fashioned police hat.

"What's this?" he asked.

"The troop sends their love. Trooper Rosco came by to check on you earlier, and he said he'd come by later with some real food for you."

"Bless him," Zeke said with a weak smile. "Not sure I could eat yet."

"Yeah, we'll wait on the doctor for that," he replied. "But the troop will be coming by to visit and make sure you don't suffer too much."

"Danke." He shook his head. The Pennsylvania Dutch seemed to be coming out more often now. "Sorry. I mean, thank you."

The troop was going to take care of its own, and Zeke appreciated that deeply, but he could still feel that emptiness that even the caring and loyalty of Troop L couldn't fill.

What's wrong with me? he thought. *Is this depression? Or something physical?*

These last few days he was supposed to be at his grandfather's house, looking at the old place he hadn't laid eyes on since he was a young teen. He was supposed to be reconnecting to his grandfather's memory, maybe even trying to sort out a little more about the man who'd gone along with the shunning of his eldest son.

"Zeke, you've got another visitor. I'll head out and give you some privacy," Chief Hernandez said. "Our prayers are all with you."

"Thank you," Zeke said. "Who's here?"

He knew the face he was hoping to see—the one that

was so battered and bruised when she had leaned over him that he'd wanted to cry. And yet it was still the most beautiful face he'd ever seen.

"Ezekiel!"

"Mamm…" He used the little remote to incline his bed up closer to a seated position, and his mother came bustling into the hospital room. "Thank you so much, Chief, for staying with him. And for everything."

"It's an honor, ma'am," the chief said. "You call me if you need anything at all."

His mother still wore her hair long and wound into a bun at the back of her head. She didn't wear a *kapp* anymore, but she did wear a handkerchief over her hair in the conservative Mennonite style. Much like the Weaverland girl had worn.

She wore a long skirt and a blouse that almost matched, but not quite.

"Son…" She stopped at the side of his bed and leaned down to kiss his forehead. "When I got a call saying you'd been shot, I thought we'd lost you!"

"*Nee*, not yet," he said with a weak smile.

"It must be the shock, but your Pennsylvania Dutch is coming back," she said.

"You sang to me in Deutsch, Mamm," he said. "You taught me to pray in Deutsch. It never went anywhere. It's my bedrock."

His mother sank down into the chair next to the bed and she took his hand in her soft hands. Her chin trembled.

"How are you feeling?" his mother asked.

"It's painful, but I'll recover."

"They had to give you a lot of blood, they said."

An image rose in his mind of Daniel Schaber's sneer.

He was a vicious man, and while Zeke hadn't been able to save every girl, he'd saved two of them. There were two women who wouldn't suffer any more because he'd planted three bullets into Schaber's chest.

"I couldn't let him take her, Mamm. I had to stop him."

Would his mother understand? Did she knew he'd killed a man? When Mamm and Daet had taken them away from the Amish life, had they known how many of those ideals would have to be cast aside in order to build an English life?

"I know you had to stop him. And I'm just glad I wasn't there to try and stop you from doing the right thing." She looked down at him earnestly. She knew he'd killed a man. He could feel it. "I've been told that those two young women are alive because of you."

"Because of God. He put me where I needed to be, and then gave me just the amount of strength I needed. To the last second."

"It's amazing how Gott works." She licked her lips. "The girls… Were they from a family we knew?"

He shook his head. "*Nee.* One was Old Order Amish from Treue, and the other was Weaverland Mennonite."

One of those women had lodged into his heart in spite of all of his attempts to keep things professional. She was extraordinary…but she was also a window into the world he'd left behind.

Mamm's eyes misted. "The police filled me in on a few details, son. I understand how wicked that man was."

In the hallway beyond the open door, he saw a group of people coming to visit someone else—regular people, someone's family most likely. Other people had communities surrounding them, and Zeke had his immediately family, and his state police colleagues. He was grateful for them, but he was missing something, too.

"I feel like every time I go through something like this, there are fewer and fewer people who understand me," Zeke said.

"You're thinking about Kinsey?" she asked.

Actually, his ex hadn't even crossed his mind. He'd been thinking about Susanna.

"I miss having a community, Mamm. I miss having people who know me and understand me. More than the ones who just work where I work. I miss a real community."

She nodded mutely.

"But that said, Mamm, no one could ever take your place. No one."

She gave his hand a squeeze. "I know that, son. Don't worry."

He'd stayed true to his family, stayed loyal to his parents. And now that Daet was gone, a part of him was wondering how much more he owed to his father. Daet wanted to give him freedom and opportunity, and Zeke had done well. But if Zeke went back to the Amish world, his mother was still shunned.

Despite it all, there were still parts of his heart that stayed lonesome, aching for something more that he'd never have on this side of the fence. He felt trapped, his heart pulling him in two directions.

His eyes were growing heavy, and his mother rose to her feet.

"You sleep, Ezekiel," she said softly. "You'll heal with rest."

Rest… Yes, that was what he longed for deep inside. He longed for the kind of rest that could last, the kind that felt like coming home, the kind that you felt when you lay down in the arms of a loving woman and could finally breathe deeply.

And as Zeke slipped back into a medicated slumber, the face that rose in his mind was of Susanna. He wasn't going to feel better until he saw her again.

THIRTEEN

The Jonestown Pennsylvania State Police department was located along Route 72. It was a single-story brick building with square windows lining each wing on either side of the front doors. There was plenty of parking in the front and at the left side of the building, but there were no buggy stalls, Susanna had noticed. There was a little manmade reservoir in the grassy yard in front of the building. Some reeds grew in some attractive little patches around it, and it seemed to serve as a drainage area for the rainy season that they had tried to pretty up a little bit.

It had been three days since her rescue, and Susanna sat in a small conference room with a Styrofoam cup of coffee with sugar and powdered creamer. She sat in front of a row of mug shots, and Trooper Bailey sat next to her. She was five months pregnant under that uniform, and Susanna had been stunned to see a pregnant wife still working such a dangerous job. But Englishers were different, it seemed, and Susanna had a whole new respect for the important work these troopers did.

"Do you recognize any of these people?" Trooper Bailey asked.

Susanna put her attention back to the row of pictures. She tapped the last one.

"This one. He called him Paul. He's the one I—" She couldn't finish what she was going to say. He was the one she nearly killed. He was the one she had accidentally pushed out of a moving vehicle. The sound of his body hitting the pavement wasn't ever going to leave her memory.

The trooper seemed to understand, because she softened her voice. "And you'd recognize him again in a lineup?"

"*Yah.* Of course."

"Good, that will help with prosecution."

"I'm glad he's not dead," she said softly.

"If he'd died, it would have been clear self-defense," the trooper said quietly. "You had the right to defend yourself. You now know what they intended to do with you."

"I'm Amish," Susanna replied. "We are pacifists. We don't take lives. The length of a life is for Gott alone to decide."

"Our job was to save you." Trooper Bailey gave her a reassuring smile. "And what happened was an accident, Susanna. Okay? And like you said, he's not dead. He's handcuffed to a hospital bed, and he's got a long and painful recovery, but he will most certainly face justice for his role in these criminal operations."

And Daniel Schaber was facing Gott already. Susanna shivered.

"Has anyone filled you in about Daniel Schaber?"

Susanna nodded. "He's dead."

"No, I meant about his criminal history and all that. I think it'll make it easier for you to make your peace with all of this," the trooper said, sitting back in her chair.

"*Nee*, not that."

"Would you like to know?"

She nodded.

"Daniel Schaber was taken into an Amish home in Ohio

as a young boy in the foster system. So he knew enough about the Amish life to know where women are vulnerable. He knew the language so he could listen in on conversations. He knew how the culture worked, and he knew where young women might be frustrated and willing to bend rules for a charming smile. Your cousin was a unique case, though. Normally he got women's trust to the point that he was able to abduct them and sell them. But for Hannah, he took more time. He wanted to keep her for himself—maybe he thought she'd be a supportive mob wife at home—something like that in his twisted mind."

"What was he doing with the women they kidnapped?" she asked. She needed to hear the worst of it.

"They were sold into a black market slave trade— shipped off to brothels or sold to private buyers who used them for whatever purposes they wanted. Mostly sexual. But with the information you were able to give us, and with Daniel dead, we're closer to shutting that operation down. They target Amish girls because they think they won't be tough enough to fight back. You proved them wrong, Susanna."

A smile touched her lips. "I didn't want to die."

"And you survived this, Susanna," Trooper Bailey said, meeting her gaze earnestly. "You survived. You fought back and you saved not only yourself, but the other girl as well. She'd be out of our reach by now if you hadn't helped her. You're a hero. Do you realize that?"

"Zeke is the hero," she said softly. "He came for me."

"Trooper Esch is a hero, too, but if you hadn't fought back and held on—"

"Sorry, I should call him Trooper Esch, shouldn't I?" She felt some heat hit her cheeks. Except Zeke was never going to be just a law enforcement officer to her.

"*Nee*, you can call me Zeke."

She startled and looked up to see Zeke standing in the open doorway. He was in a pair of jeans and a t-shirt and he had a sling that held his arm against his chest. He met Susanna's gaze with a smile.

"Trooper Bailey, do you think I could have a moment with Susanna?" Zeke asked.

"Of course." The trooper stood up and cast a smile between them. "Take your time."

Trooper Bailey headed out of the room, and Susanna stood up. It was so wonderful to see Zeke standing there that she felt like she could cry.

"Are you all right?" she asked softly.

Zeke crossed the room and looked down at her. He put a finger under her chin and tipped her face up. He narrowed his gaze, looking her face over carefully.

"Your face is healing, but it looks awfully painful."

She hadn't even thought of her own injuries compared to his. He released her chin and she looked down.

"It'll heal, they say," she said.

"It'll heal," he agreed.

When he was lying on the ground, he'd promised to kiss her when he saw her next, and the thought of that kiss made some heat hit her cheeks, but Zeke didn't seem to be making a move toward that.

She looked up again, and found his warm brown eyes moving over her face.

"Are the bruises that upsetting?" she asked.

He nodded. "*Yah*. But you're alive, and these bruises mean you fought back." He touched her cheek tenderly.

"I promised to kiss you," he said softly. "But that would be wrong of me to do. I'm in a position of authority, you see, and you're recovering from a very traumatic experience."

"Oh." That was a relief. Or it should be. She blinked a couple of times to clear her vision from some welling tears. "Susanna…"

"*Nee*, it's okay," she said. Because he was right of course. She was Amish, and she should not be toying with a romantic relationship with an Englisher. It was wrong. "You'll always be very special to me, Zeke. Always. But I'm Amish and you aren't."

"*Yah.*" He nodded. "I won't take a kiss that doesn't rightfully belong to me. That belongs to the man you marry."

She nodded. The man she married… She couldn't imagine trusting herself to any man other than Zeke. That would take a very long time to change, and she was already considered an old maid. Maybe Zeke would be the man she cherished in her heart—the one she'd loved, even though she couldn't be with him.

Many unmarried women had memories like that stored up. She could join them—having tasted love, but having it remain unrequited.

She looked into his eyes. They seemed to be filled with pain and longing.

"Just so you know," he whispered, "I wish I could keep that promise. I do." Then he took a step back, opening a gulf between them. "Where will you go now that this is over?"

"I'm staying with my aunt and uncle for now," she said. "My family thinks I should go stay with my brother in Ohio. He's arranging some travel plans to come get me."

"Ohio…"

"It's far away," she conceded. "But I have to submit to my family's wishes. They want to keep me safe."

"They love you," he breathed.

"*Yah.*"

The word *love* hung between them, and Susanna wondered what Zeke felt for her. Was she being naive? Because she did love this man. He'd put his life on the line for her. He'd been willing to die to rescue her. But maybe that was just his job. Maybe she wasn't any more special than Holly or any other person he'd saved in the years of his work as a detective.

"I'm getting another couple of personal days," Zeke said. "I still need to go to my grandfather's house and have a look around at my inheritance."

"I'm glad you can do that," she said.

"How much time do you have before your brother arrives from Ohio?" he asked.

"A few days."

"Do you want to come with me to see the house? Just for a day? I could have you back at your aunt and uncle's place before bedtime." He dropped his gaze then. "Please feel free to say no if you'd rather not. This is a personal request, and if you would rather—"

As if it were even possible for her to refuse him after all he'd done for her. She would be his friend, and she would support him in any way she could, since that was all that was available to them.

"I want to come, Zeke," she broke in. "I want to see his house—your house."

"I guess it'll be mine until I figure out what to do with it," he said. There was an unsettled look in his eye.

"*Yah*, I'll come with you," she said. "It'll be okay. Your Amish family might be more accepting than you think."

He smiled then. "Okay. *Danke*."

It would be so much easier if she weren't in love with this unreachable man. But she could cherish one more day alone with him.

And then real life would have to reign.

* * *

That afternoon, Zeke and Susanna stood on the solid wooden porch in front of his grandfather's front door.

Side doors were for friends and family. Front doors were for guests…or for inheriting grandsons who only had the one key. They hadn't given him a side door key—just one to the front. That had felt like a message in itself.

But the old house was so familiar still that it gave his heart a squeeze. This porch had been rebuilt, but it had the same bench swing on one end, the same old metal Crisco can filled with dirt that his grandparents had used for a doorstop.

He unlocked the door and Susanna stood back to let him go inside first. But she followed him in close behind, their footsteps echoing on the wooden floor. He looked around the sitting room. There were wooden chairs set up in a circle around the room, a pedal sewing machine on a table right in front of the big front window. Mammi, or Grandma, had died years ago, but Dawdie, or Grandpa, refused to move that old sewing machine. It had been a fixture for him, a touchstone with his late wife's memory.

"This is a beautiful home," Susanna said.

"*Yah*, it is," he agreed. "It's the same as I remember it, too. Dawdie didn't change anything."

"No use changing what works." She cast him a small smile, and he chuckled softly.

"You're right. He would have said that. It's the Amish way."

"I think you're still Amish at heart, Zeke," she said.

Was he? He felt like he was, but being Amish was about more than ideals and upbringing. The Amish were their community. An Amish man did not live in isolation.

They wandered through the kitchen—a simple room

with a few dishes and two pots, one frying pan. There were drawers filled with ladles and cooking utensils, but they didn't seem to have been used in a long time. His grandfather had been cooking simply for himself on a big, black woodstove.

"I remember having huge family gatherings in this house," Zeke said quietly. "Before Mammi died. Aunts and uncles, cousins, second and third cousins…people would come from miles around and we'd have a massive cookout. The women would make fifty or sixty pies, they'd bring huge buckets of potato salad, and we'd have haystacks, and we'd put on a corn roast…" The food seemed to top his childhood memories. But it represented something, too. "We belonged together."

He looked over at Susanna. He could see past those bruises now to the woman with her compassionate gaze.

"We had dinners like that before my siblings all left, too," she said. "But times change, I guess."

"We aren't so different, are we?" he asked. "We both wish we had that belonging again."

She nodded. "I suppose we do."

He caught her hand in his warm grip and they ambled together down a hallway. There was a closed door, and Zeke pushed it open with a creak.

"Dawdie's study," he said.

A big desk dominated the room, bookshelves behind it. There were some piles of books and papers spread over the desktop. Dawdie had always been a reader. He'd wanted to write a history of the Amish in their area, and he'd been gathering information for as long as Zeke could remember. He'd never started writing, though. It had all been in his head.

"I remember the smell of this room," he said. The scent

of paper and book bindings, and the soft scent of the over-grown lilac bush outside the window. It smelled like home in some deep part of his heart.

Susanna released his hand and turned around the room. She paused at a framed picture on the wall, cocked her head to one side to examine it more closely.

"That's well-done," she said.

He joined her and looked at the charcoal drawing of a running horse. He knew it was charcoal, because he'd done the picture and had given it to his grandmother. But here it was framed in his *dawdie*'s office—a place of honor on the wall next to the big calendar.

"I drew that," he breathed.

All those years away, and his grandfather had kept this memento of a grandson belonging to parents who had left the faith.

"He kept it," he murmured.

"You drew that?"

"As a boy."

"It's very good," she said.

He cast her a wobbly smile. "I thought they'd wiped me from their hearts. I thought they'd forgotten us."

And then he remembered something else his grandfather used to do, and he went to the big desk and pulled open the top drawer. There was a piece of paper folded up in quarters, and he carefully unfolded it and smoothed it out.

It was a list—names written in small, tight handwriting. Names upon names—some with dates jotted next to them. Some with a note next to them that said "answered."

"What is it?" Susanna asked.

"My *dawdie*'s prayer list," he said.

But he had to see if he was right, and he ran his finger down the list of names. His grandmother's name topped the list, his father's name was there, too, being their son, and his mother's, and then he saw his own name written out in that neat, tight script. Ezekiel Esch.

Dawdie had them all on his prayer list. Dawdie had been praying for them…for him. They were not forgotten in his grandfather's most personal moments when he bowed before Herr Gott and prayed for his family.

Tears misted his eyes as he looked around that office, with the window partially blocked by that overgrown lilac bush. It wasn't just the familiar scent, or the memories attached to these old rooms. He knew that he had to come home. It was time.

Susanna slipped her hand into his and he closed his fingers around hers and looked down at her tenderly.

"I love you," he whispered. It was a concession—something he'd been trying not to admit. But it was true, and it was time to get back to those fundamental truths inside of himself.

"I love you, too," she whispered.

"*Yah?* You sure?"

She nodded, but there was sadness in her eyes, too. She didn't think they had a future, whatever they felt.

"Susanna, what if I came back?" he asked. "What if I didn't sell this house, and I kept it? What if I came back to the faith and joined the community?"

"You mean, become Amish again?" she asked, a stunned look on her face.

He nodded. "I've had this hole in my heart for years—and I couldn't fill it. I missed community and faith, and family."

"What about your *mamm*? She's shunned. You'd never be able to see her again, Zeke."

"Daet is gone, and if she rejoined the faith, too, all would be forgiven for her. My siblings were never baptized, so they wouldn't be held back from visiting."

"Are you being serious?" she breathed.

"I'm deadly serious." He touched her bruised cheek gently. "I didn't kiss you before because I didn't have a right to it… but I love you, and you love me. I know that coming back and getting baptized would take time, but would you wait for me?"

"Wait for…" She looked up, breath bated. He wasn't being very clear, was he?

"I want to marry you," he said. "I want to come back, become Amish again, and I want to court you properly and make you my wife. That's what I want."

Tears welled in her eyes, and he looked up into the most beautiful face in the world. She nodded, her chin trembling.

"*Yah,* I will marry you, Zeke."

Zeke tugged her a little closer and slid his arms around her. She felt perfect there—slim and warm and beautiful. He dipped his head down and caught her lips with his. Their breath mingled, and he finally allowed himself to kiss her with all the pent-up emotion inside of him. She twined her arms around his neck, and he wished he could stay that way and never leave her arms again.

But there were plans to make, and a bishop to become reacquainted with. There was a home to prepare, vows to give to the faith and to the community, and finally with all of his heart, vows to give to Susanna, too.

He'd come home…right into the arms of the only woman for him. And for the first time in decades, he felt peace circle around him and settle over him like a mantle.

He couldn't wait to make her his wife.

EPILOGUE

Susanna invited her siblings to her wedding that took place at her and Zeke's house in the Felder community. This would be their home together—the house that had belonged to Zeke's grandparents.

Susanna's family had all been shocked at her quick engagement to a cop, and they'd rushed back to Treue to make sure that she was okay. But then they met Zeke, and once they saw Susanna with her fiancé together, they understood. She'd met the love of her life, and Zeke was coming back to the Amish fold. It wasn't scary, after all. It made sense.

Susanna stayed with her aunt and uncle while Zeke took a baptismal class at his church district. The bishop, now a very old man, was grateful for his return. He'd told Zeke that his grandfather had been praying he'd come back all that time, and the bishop truly believed that Gott had answered.

Their wedding was a simple affair—simpler than most Amish weddings. They only had two hundred people in attendance, both communities coming together to celebrate their vows to each other. Troop L was invited, too, of course. They didn't come in uniform, and the Amish folks shyly said hello. They knew what Zeke had done— how he'd saved one of their own, and how he'd come home again. So the Amish people made sure that the Englishers understood the words spoken, and they showed them their own gratitude the best way they knew how—with food.

Zeke wasn't part of the police force anymore. He'd given his resignation so that he could come back to live Amish, and Susanna knew what that meant to him. It was a sacrifice, but it was also a testament to his dedication.

The women cooked and baked to feed everyone, and Susanna and Zeke got to sit together in the *eck*—the corner where the head table was set up. And every time Susanna looked over at Zeke with his gentle eyes and those strong hands that reminded her of his competence and his tenderness, she felt a wave of love and gratitude.

Gott had filled her heart to overflowing.

After the speeches and prayers, after wedding cake and a big meal, Zeke's old boss approached them. Susanna assumed he was saying goodbye.

"Could I speak with you alone?" Chief Hernandez asked.

Susanna made to step back, but the chief stopped her.

"You, too, ma'am," he said. "You're married now, and this will affect you both."

"What's going on?" Zeke asked, putting a protective hand on Susanna's back. "I can't come back to work for the force, sir."

"It's not that," the chief replied. "Although you know you'd always be welcome back. The thing is, this human trafficking ring is big and ugly, and I'm sorry to bring the subject up on such a beautiful day, but we at the state police want to infiltrate their organization. In order to do that, we need to send some officers into these local Amish communities under cover."

Susanna held her breath. Was Chief Hernandez asking Zeke to go under cover? Because that would not be allowed.

They had to stay in good standing with their community and this was not the way to do it. He'd promised her…

"What do you need from me?" Zeke asked.

"We'd like to rent your house in Treue," the chief replied. "And perhaps ask you folks a few questions about dress and manners. That's all. We'd pay well for the space, and maybe you'd be willing to speak with the bishops in both districts to see if they'd be supportive."

Susanna nearly wilted with relief. She looked up at Zeke and found his questioning gaze locked on her. She nodded.

"We could talk to the bishops and get back to you."

"That's all I can ask," the chief said. "Thank you. And congratulations to you. May you have many years of happiness together."

When the chief took his leave, Zeke pulled her close against him and leaned his cheek against her neat *kapp*.

"I won't be making any decisions without you, Susanna," he said. "Never worry about that."

She nodded, and as she looked out at the chatting, happy groups of people, the setting sun outside splashing gold and rose hues over the Pennsylvania farmland, Susanna sent up a prayer for blessing on their marriage, and for success for the state police.

They only enjoyed this peace and beauty because of the Englishers who protected them, and she was grateful for all that Gott had given them on this very first day of married life.

"I love you, Zeke," she said.

Such simple words for such deep feeling. She had the rest of her life to explore it.

* * * * *

Dear Reader,

This is my second Love Inspired Suspense book, and I am really enjoying adding some danger into my romances! Going forward, you will notice that I'm writing both regular Amish romance with Love Inspired, and Amish suspense stories with Love Inspired Suspense. I hope you'll try out all of my books. You might discover that you really like my other offerings, too.

If you'd like to connect with me, you can find me on my website at PatriciaJohns.com as well as on social media. I'm always thrilled to hear from my readers, and I'm sure to respond if you reach out.

If you enjoy this story, I hope you'll leave a review! Reviews really help an author to get the word out about her books, and I am always eternally grateful for every review that is posted. In fact, if you leave a review and let me know about it, I'll say thank you personally!

Patricia

[illegible]

Get up to 4 Free Books!

We'll send you 2 free books from each series you try
PLUS a free Mystery Gift.

Both the **Love Inspired®** and **Love Inspired® Suspense** series feature compelling novels filled with inspirational romance, faith, forgiveness and hope.

YES! Please send me 2 FREE novels from the Love Inspired or Love Inspired Suspense series and my FREE gift (gift is worth about $10 retail). I may cancel anytime by emailing ReaderServiceInfo@Harlequin.com or by calling 1-800-873-8635. If I don't cancel, I will receive 6 brand-new Love Inspired Larger-Print books or Love Inspired Suspense Larger-Print books every month and be billed just $7.19 each in the U.S. or $7.99 each in Canada. That is a savings of 20% off the cover price. It's quite a bargain! Shipping and handling is just 75¢ per book in the U.S. and $1.75 per book in Canada.* I understand that accepting the free books and gift places me under no obligation to buy anything—they are mine to keep for free no matter what I decide.

Choose one:
- ☐ **Love Inspired Larger-Print** (122/322 BPA G3CD)
- ☐ **Love Inspired Suspense Larger-Print** (107/307 BPA G3CD)
- ☐ **Or Try Both!** (122/322 & 107/307 BPA G3CE)

Name (please print)

Address _______ Apt. #

City _______ State/Province _______ Zip/Postal Code

Email: Please check this box ☐ if you would like to receive newsletters and promotional emails from Harlequin Enterprises ULC and its affiliates. You can unsubscribe anytime.

Mail to the **Harlequin Reader Service:**
IN U.S.A.: P.O. Box 1341, Buffalo, NY 14240-8531
IN CANADA: P.O. Box 603, Fort Erie, Ontario L2A 5X3

Want to explore our other series or interested in ebooks? Visit www.ReaderService.com or call 1-800-873-8635.

LIRLIS2603